Convicted Love

Convicted Love

KRISTEE L. JORDAN

authorHOUSE®

AuthorHouse™
1663 Liberty Drive
Bloomington, IN 47403
www.authorhouse.com
Phone: 1-800-839-8640

First published by AuthorHouse   05/04/2011

ISBN: 978-1-4634-0511-3 (sc)
ISBN: 978-1-4634-0512-0 (dj)
ISBN: 978-1-4634-2555-5 (ebk)

Library of Congress Control Number: 2011908209

Printed in the United States of America

With thanks to God for this wonderful gift of writing.

To my family: thanks for your love and support.
I love you all.

"Forgiveness is a powerful weapon. Use it!"
—Kristee L. Jordan

Chapter One

I never knew that a child could be born into tragedy and grow into triumph. After all I was never supposed to make it to adulthood. I remember how it all happened deep in the south where the sweltering heat knows no mercy and the people where all acquainted with one another. I remember the evil thing that happened in that house that I never thought I would return to. I remember all that I had endured in my childhood home. I also knew in order for me to fully embrace womanhood I would have to make peace with my childhood. I never thought I'd see the day when I would make my way back home to this little town that held my past. But my childhood memory of this place would not start out so tragically. Ironically my first recollection of this journey would start in church as a twelve year old girl.

Sundays were supposed to be relaxing days. So why didn't I feel relaxed? Worse yet, why did I feel like I was working in church? I was getting tired of trying to keep up with Pastor Jacobs. I mean, *Slow down, Pastor. I'm trying to keep up with you. Does anybody know what time it is?*

Grandma Bean snapped her fingers at me, trying to get my attention. "Micah Bean, do you hear me, gal? Micah, stop daydreaming in church. Don't you know the Lord sees you? Can't blame the child, but blame that fast mama of yours for your attitude!"

Grandma Bean had a way of getting my attention. She was a good woman now, but she ran a bootleg hole on the block back in the day. She stopped when I was born. Now she still cursed a little bit, but she just asked God to forgive her all the time. I guess he forgave her, 'cause she was old and still here.

"Grandma Bean, what time is it?" I asked in a very exhausted tone.

"Micah, for the last time," she replied, "stop timing church. It's over when the Lord says so!"

"But Grandma Bean, I'm hungry. You know church makes me hungry."

Grandma Bean gave me a serious look. "Micah, do you want me to thump you on your nose in the Lord's house?"

I slouched down in the church pew and folded my arms in discontent. "No, ya wrinkled oldie-but-goody." I had a bad habit of mumbling things under my breath, thinking I wouldn't get caught.

Grandma Bean sat up quickly and clutched her pocketbook. "Wait a minute. I know you didn't just get smart with me. Girl, I will bust you up in here! And sit up and pay attention!"

I slowly eased my body to an upright position while straightening out my skirt with one hand and massaging out the pew crease on the side of my cheek with the other. "Man, I can't win for losing."

Grandma Bean waited for me to position myself correctly, folding her arms and tapping her feet as if we were in a standoff that she was sure to win. "Micah, stand your lazy butt up for the altar call! Don't you know someone might get saved today? God needs your support to call the unsaved down the aisle. Just because you're twelve, don't mean you ain't accountable."

Oh, Lord, hurry up and come take me away. Forget about Calgon; I want you to come down and take me now! I looked at Grandma Bean as she began to hold out her arms and seemed to sway them back and forth, like she was surrendering or giving up something.

Grandma Bean was always emotional during the altar call. "Raise your arms, child! Close your eyes. Can't you hear Pastor Jacobs praying for lost souls to be saved?" Tears began to flow down her butterscotch-colored cheeks.

Now, Pastor Tony Jacobs was a good man, and he could pray up something, do you hear me? I remember when this one lady couldn't walk. Boy, he grabbed hold of her legs, and the next thing you know, she was up and running around. Then there was that time he made Mama vomit up black stuff; they say the demons came out of her, you know. Well, they musta come back, because she was a-drinking and cussing the next day.

Everyone in the church always shouted "Amen" when it was time to go. "Amen!" said the church people.

Grandma Bean grabbed my arm and her pocketbook. "Let's go, Micah. We better get home and start dinner 'fore your mother come home." No matter what, Grandma Bean always wanted to please Mama. Grandma Bean always tried to make her feel welcome and comfortable when she came by the house. After all, Mama did grow up there.

I was never happy to see Mama, especially after all the chaos and embarrassment she caused Grandma Bean. Mama was always getting herself into trouble, and Grandma Bean was always willing to spend money or defend Mama's reputation in order to help her out of a situation. I wished Mama would just leave me and Grandma Bean alone. We were perfectly fine all by ourselves!

I heard the rumbling of pots and pans against the stove top all the way from upstairs. The aroma of a home cooked meal lured me downstairs to the kitchen, and I parked my behind at the front of the table and begin to dive into the delicious sacrifice that Grandma Bean had prepared for me. I loved Grandma Bean's cooking! Um-um good . . . fried country steak, rice, peas, corn bread, sun-brewed tea, and an apple pie for dinner.

Grandma Bean was taking her time eating her food, as if she was trying to eat slowly in order to wait for Mama to arrive. I couldn't help but finish my dinner a little earlier than Grandma Bean. If there's one thing I know, Mama never arrives on time when she is supposed to. "This was great Grandma. Can I have some apple pie?"

Grandma Bean put down her fork and went to the kitchen window and looked outside. She let out a big smile and headed to the door. But before she could open the door, Mama had already let herself in, and she did not come to dinner alone this time. Mama came shuffling around the corner in her wore-out loafers she was wearing. Mama looked at me as if she was happy to see me and came straight to the kitchen, bypassing Grandma Bean's open-arm hug. "Micah, hey, baby, give your Mama some sugar."

Mama bent over to kiss me and reeked of alcohol. She looked awful! My mother was a very big woman. I mean, some women are big here and some there, but my mama was big everywhere. Mama was a brown-skinned color like me. She had been a drunk for as long as I had known her. She always wore tight clothing and fake hair. Her name is Irish. People around here call here Wild Irish Rose; that's her favorite drink. She could drink any man under the table. She weighed over four hundred pounds, and it was no coincidence how much alcohol she could hold.

But ya know, Mama always could keep a man. For as long as she'd been my mama, she always had some drunken man by her side. Now she had a new man. People on the street called him Woody. I heard Woody was a big-time pimp and dope dealer. He was what every pimp dreamed of being—rich and high, twenty-four seven, and living off some poor women with low self-esteem. Woody drove a fancy, black BMW, and the license plate on the back read "MAN WORKN." Now you know that don't make no type of sense! How he gonna be a man working when he a man pimping? Plus, he was actually kind of cute: slim, tall, brown hair, blue eyes, white, and . . . it just didn't make sense at all, the two of them together.

Woody was staring at me with a smirk on his face. And I was staring back at him. You not gonna stare me down in my own home! Mama noticed the interaction between us and abruptly interrupted. "Micah, this is Woody. Woody this is Micah, my daughter I was telling you about."

Woody walked over to me and held out his hand for a handshake. I just stared at his hand, because I wasn't sure what he wanted me to do with it. I mean, I wasn't going to shake this man's hand. I didn't know him!

Woody cleared his throat, withdrew his hand, and placed both hands inside his pockets before speaking. "Um, wow. Irish said you were pretty. Had no idea you were that pretty. I have a feeling we are going to be family. I don't have any kids, but I

5

always wanted a daughter. I don't think your mama can give me any on account of she's so big and fat." Woody let out a big laugh. Woody's laugh sounded like a hyena.

Woody noticed I wasn't laughing. He took a step toward me as if to try to hug me, and I took two steps back. The nerve of this guy, coming into our home and insulting my own mother! I was the only one who could do that! Grandma Bean looked shocked, and Mama looked embarrassed that her man just downed her in front of her family. The phone rang, and Grandma Bean went over to pick it up.

Woody cleared his throat again and glided his fingers through his hair. "It's all fun and games; me and Irish joke like that all the time. Irish knows I love her."

Mama had a look on her face as if she didn't know what to say. Then she cleared her throat and started fumbling with the snug shirt she had on. "Yeah, Micah," she said, "Woody is always trying to play with me like that. I'm sure you too are going to have fun once you get to know each other."

Mama looked down and then back at Woody as if to see if that was okay, what she just said. Then Mama looked at me and gave a big smile. I knew something wasn't right with Mama and him. "I'm not too sure about that, Mama," I said.

I was saved by Grandma Bean when she yelled, "Micah, telephone. It sounds like Shana."

I went into the hallway where Grandma Bean had gone to answer the phone. Grandma Bean motioned for me with her hand to go upstairs to talk. I caught Grandma Bean out of the corner of my eye going back into the kitchen where Mama and Woody were. That wasn't good. I knew Grandma Bean was going to give Mama a piece of her mind. I ran upstairs, fast as I could. And then it started. I heard Mama and Grandma Bean yelling. I closed the door, jumped on the bed, and yelled, "I got it, Grandma Bean!" I had no time to hear what was going on downstairs.

Then I heard the front door slam and Grandma Bean stomping up the stairs to her room. "Girl, don't forget you washing dishes tonight!" Grandma Bean yelled.

"All right, Grandma."

The coast was clear. I knew Shana had something to say that she wasn't supposed to. After all, she was my best friend and would tell me everything. "Hey, Shana, what's up?"

Shana was every mother's nightmare. She was always getting into trouble with kids for stirring up gossip. Everyone at school called her "Channel 2 News," because she was the gossip queen. She knew all and told all, but the girl was scared of everything. Scared to eat, scared to sleep, scared to use the bathroom alone, scared of the dark—but always in trouble behind something.

"Micah, have you seen the new girl that moved down the street from you?"

"What new girl?" I asked.

"That red-headed, light-skinned girl?" she said in a nervous voice.

No, I haven't seen anyone move in, and Grandma Bean didn't mention anybody new to me. Sometimes Shana could act just plain crazy! "Shana, you been smoking?"

"No, Micah. I mean for real, though; she just moved into the neighborhood. They call her Cherish," she said adamantly.

"Cherish? What kind of name is that?" I said.

"A name that will steal Linwood from you!" she replied in a stern voice.

Linwood was my so-called boyfriend. He was older than me, and he'd failed one grade before. Linwood was thirteen, but he was still in the sixth grade. He'd asked me to be his girlfriend last Friday. He wrote me a note. It said, *Do you like me? Check yes or no.* So I just checked *yes*, because he was bigger than all the other kids at school.

"Shana, tomorrow at school, point her out to me," I said. "I need to know who she is."

Shana hesitated for a moment. "Yeah, Micah, I thought you would like to know who your competition was."

Shana knows me too well. I don't know what would happen if we ever were separated. And I hated to admit when she was right. "Save it, Channel 2. Just do as I say and not as I do! Well, I got to go, Shana. Meet me in front of my house tomorrow before school. Goodnight!"

Shana dropped the phone and picked it back up. I could hear her struggling with the receiver. I giggled under my breath. Shana was so clumsy sometimes! "Goodnight, Micah," she replied.

The next morning, I was up extra early. The anticipation was killing me. Who was this new girl, and why did she have to move into my neighborhood? There were plenty of other neighborhoods she could've moved into. A million questions were running through my mind, as well as concerns. Would she like Linwood? Was he her type? Nah, she couldn't possibly like Linwood. She was too light-skinned for him.

Would all the boys in school like her? What was gonna happen to me and Shana's cutie-pie reputations? We're supposed to be the finest girls in school. We are supposed to have it going on, and besides, all the boys love to grab our butts anyway. What if her butt was bigger than mine? That's really the only thing I got going for me. I never knew I even had a butt until Shana pointed it out to me. *Okay, okay,* I thought. *Let me weight my options here. Cherish is lighter than me, and probably has good hair. Wait a minute; wait just one minute. Cherish is lighter than me with good red hair. Now, normally, light-skinned people don't have big butts. They have little butts with little noses.*

Grandma Bean hated when I was running late. I could hear her calling me. "Micah, hurry up and get down here 'fore you be late for school!"

Ugh! If I could just put on those fitted jeans. There! All zipped up now and ready to go. "Yes, Grandma, I'm coming," I yelled back at her.

I put on my jacket, slapped my butt for good luck, and ran downstairs. Well, butt don't fail me now!

Grandma Bean gave me lunch money and a kiss on the cheek before I headed outside. I could see Shana waiting on her bike in front of our country home. School was literally a fifteen-minute bike ride, and we could ride our bikes to school. But Grandma Bean would only let us go if Shana and I rode our bikes to and from school together.

It was another sunny day in the south, and blue skies and warm weather made great conditions to ride a bike to school. Shana was all bright-eyed and bushy-tailed with her chocolate-covered skin and bushy hair. She was a pretty girl. Her parents were Jamaica-born, wealthy, educated folks. Grandma Bean always thought Shana was a good friend for me to have, although she has no idea how much Shana gossiped! I just knew deep down that Shana had something she was itching to say this morning.

"What's up, Micah? You kind of late, ain't you?"

I hopped on my bike as if I was calm, cool, and collected. "Anyway," I said, "this is just another day at school. I'm not worried about anything or *anyone.*"

Shana started peddling her bicycle as if she hadn't heard a thing. But I knew she'd heard me. I started peddling behind her and said in a louder voice, to make sure she heard me, "Shana, I'm not worried about nobody stealing Linwood from me."

We rode our bikes across the gravel and unto the bike path on the way to school. Shana slowed down her peddling and rode up beside me, then blurted out, "Not yet, but you will! I've seen her, but you haven't. I know what she looks like, Micah." Then she sped up her peddling to get in front of me on the bike path.

"Shana," I said, "you need to work on your self-esteem, child. I mean, really though, stalking the new girl and trying to make sure she's not our competition. Don't you have better things to do with your time?"

Shana sped up her peddling again, flicking dirt from the back of her bike wheel and said, "You can play dumb if you want to. You mark my word, the girl is trouble! I can see it in her eyes!"

I slowed down my speed while gliding into the bike ramp at school. I giggled under my breath. Shana had a way of exaggerating, but that's why we call her Channel 2 News. There was dust on the back of both of our shoes from the bike ride. Shana and I locked up our bikes and cleaned the dirt off the backs of our heels. The cafeteria was the first part of our usual routine. Besides, Grandma Bean said it was the most important meal of the day.

Linwood always met me for breakfast every morning at school. Sometimes I called him Linny for short, depending on how I felt. I guess he was kind of cute in his own way. I mean, everybody knew we were going together. He always carried my breakfast tray, and he was the only guy in sixth grade with a gold tooth. He often reminded me of a mini-thug.

"Hey, baby girl, did you miss me?"

"Why you ain't call me last night, Linny?" I replied.

I knew Linwood would make up some excuse. He wasn't much of a phone person. The last time we'd talked on the phone, he fell asleep. "I didn't want to wake you up from your beauty sleep, and besides, that gave me all the more reason to get here early to see your pretty face."

I smiled because Linwood had a way with words. Normally during breakfast, we all cracked jokes on each other. Linwood was talking about me and Shana's dusty shoes. We were having a good time, when Shana reached over to me and thumped my elbow.

"Girl, is you crazy?" I asked.

Shana pointed to a girl standing in front of the cafeteria holding her breakfast tray. "Look, I told you she was coming today," she said.

Sure enough, there she was. Indeed, she was very pretty, but there was something quite different about her . . . almost mysterious. Cherish was very red. I mean, everything was red, including her eyebrows. She was very petite and really looked self-confident. I could tell she wasn't scared of her new school. Her hair was long and thick. Her clothes were perfect—not a wrinkle or crease. She walked with such poise and grace. Every eye turned and looked at her, including Linwood's. She headed straight for our table, and everyone I was sitting with seemed to welcome her through their body language.

"Is anyone sitting here?" she asked.

I couldn't deny there was an open space right next to me. "No," I replied in a not-so-nice voice.

Shana slid over slightly and pointed to a spot between us. "You can sit down next to me and Micah," she said.

Shana pointed to the table next to her and gave me a look as if I should have known better. I smacked my lips and tried to get a grip on everything that was going on inside of me. How could Shana ask my soon-to-be enemy to have a seat next to me? I was going to kill that girl when we got home.

I decided I should make conversation to show that I am a "bigger person," as Grandma Bean would say. "So what's your name?"

Cherish had on a pair of jeans and T-shirt. She sat down and immediately took a bite of her peaches. I guess she didn't think I would ask her questions so quickly. "My name is Cherish, but my family calls me Cherry," she replied while covering her mouth so that we could not see her chew her food.

Cherish took a big gulp and swallowed her food. "What's y'all name?"

Linwood stood up and held out his hand. "I'm Linwood, but you can call me Linny, baby girl."

I stood up and slapped his hand back, "No the hell she can't!"

Linwood slowly took his seat, while Shana and Linwood's friends said, "Oooh." I looked at Linwood as if he had lost his everlasting mind. Nobody called him Linny but me, and I would be a fool in hell before she started calling him by his nickname. Then I rolled my eyes at him and directed my attention toward her.

I held out my hand to shake hers as if to let her know I was the head girl in charge. "Well, my name is Micah."

Cherish took another gulp of her peaches and replied, "Micah, I know you. Well, I seen you in church on Sunday."

I was puzzled. "That's funny," I said. "I didn't see you in church."

Cherish gobbled down the last of her cereal. "We arrived kind of late but managed to get a seat in the back."

I let out a snicker of laughter under my breath. "Oh, so you a backseat Christian?"

Cherish wiped her mouth. "A backseat what?"

"You know, people who come to church late just to sit in the back of the church," I replied.

I knew I must have ruffled her feathers, because her pale skin began to turn red.

"Didn't I just say we got to church late?" she said.

I smacked my lips to her response. "Whatever you say."

Cherish looked stunned. "Yeah, the same to ya!" she said.

The tension between Cherish and me was so thick you could cut it with a knife. Shana looked as if she didn't know what to do. Linwood acted as if he didn't care anyway. So I decided to change the subject. I wasn't going to let this girl ruin our routine.

Then Shana blurted out, "Hey, you guys, who wants to meet at the playground after school?"

The playground was our hangout place after school. That's where all the action took place. That's also were Linwood beat up the underclassman.

Shana looked at me with a crazy look. "Shana," I said, "you know we usually meet around four o'clock. Now what would make today any different?"

I was trying to figure out Shana's motives. Maybe Shana was trying to invite Cherish to our hangout and get to know her a little better before I made my final judgment that she was indeed after Linwood. "I figured we could invite Cherish to come a long with us," said Shana. "Micah, maybe we can show her around."

Shana anxiously waited for my reply. I took a deep breath and directed my attention toward Cherish. "Cherish, dear, do you have any plans after school?"

Cherish opened her mouth to reply, so I quickly interrupted her.

"Great, Cherish. You can meet us after school at the playground." I had a smirk on my face like a chessy cat.

Cherish looked very mad. "Sure, Micah," she replied. "I will be very glad to hang with you guys after school. Very glad, indeed."

Cherish had to know this was going to be an interview. I had to know her intentions one way or another. "Good girl, Cherish. You need to consider yourself privileged. Not too many new kids get to hang with this crew."

Cherish put down her fork and looked at me. "I will be there, Micah. I promise." She smirked back.

The bell rang loudly. Breakfast was over and it was time for homeroom. Linwood gathered up my books, and we began to leave the cafeteria. "Oh, and Cherry, dear, don't be late!" I giggled under my breath. I'd called her Cherry. Now, how did she feel about that?

I smiled and slowly began to walk away. I could feel her looking at me. *Yes*, I thought. *Now she knows who the boss around school is.* The rest of the day seemed to drag on forever. My patience was wearing very thin with these schoolteachers. I mean, what is the purpose of school anyway? I would like to know who made the rule that we had to be in school this long?

I must have daydreamed through the entire day, because before I knew it, the end of the day was there. Shana always met me by the swings, and Linwood always met me by my locker. Neither Shana nor Linwood were around. I walked toward the monkey bars, and guess who I saw. Cherish was there. Cherish was there on time too. "I see you got here on time, huh?"

Cherish folded her arms and looked at me. "Yeah, Micah," she replied. "I found my way around okay. I have a message from Linwood and Shana."

So, that was what abandonment felt like, I thought. "Linwood and Shana?" I asked. I must've looked surprised; this was her first day in school and already she was the personal message-relater.

Cherish appeared perfectly comfortable. "Yeah, um Linwood got suspended for beating up a guy named Travis, and Shana's mother came to pick her up early. She said something about needing new dance shoes. So I guess it's just me and you."

Well, now, this was quite disappointing. "Yeah, me and you," I replied.

I didn't know exactly what to say to her alone. I felt awkward and uneasy. Cherish was what they called a red-boned black girl. I mean, she even had red hair! But I had to admit she was pretty, and her hair was long and straight. She looked cool and collected. The clouds suddenly grew dark, and I started to hear the roar of thunder. Cherish and I both looked up at the sky. One raindrop hit my nose, then another, and another, until it began to pour down rain.

"Let's get out of here, Micah!" Cherish shouted.

My jeans and shirt were getting soaking wet. I didn't want my long thick hair to get wet, or it would curl up from its straight hairstyle. Grandma Bean would be mad, because she took a lot of time and hair grease to do it. "I can't go home," I said. "My grandma's not off work yet. That's why I usually stay after school or chill over at Shana's house. Shana went home, though, so I guess I'll go to my grandma's job and wait till she gets off work."

Cherish grabbed my arm, and we took shelter next to the school building. Everyone was gone by now, and we were almost fully wet. "Well, you can always come to my house," Cherish said. "I mean, that is, if you can stand to be around me. My foster mom won't mind."

"I don't really have a choice, Cherish," I replied.

Cherish and I made a fast break for our bicycles and hopped on them. I had to swallow my pride, and besides, it was raining. I didn't want to stay there for much longer. I hopped on my bike, and Cherish led the way. We tried to beat the rain, but we were no match for Mother Nature, of course. The muddy shoes, wet pants, and drenched hair were proof that Mother Nature had won this battle. We peddled as fast as we could until we came upon Cherish's huge, southern-style brick home. She motioned for me to pull my bike into the garage after hers.

We left our shoes at the door and tiptoed up to her bedroom. She had all sorts of porcelain dolls and a big canopy bed with matching pink sheets. I didn't want to touch anything, because I was afraid I might break something. She had all the latest Christian CDs and a huge floor-model TV, but she acted as if none of those things mattered. "Your room is nice," I said. "Man, I would love to have this room." I couldn't deny it was a beautiful room.

Cherish seemed pleased that I was opening up to her in conversation, but to me, this didn't make us cool. She went into her own personal bathroom for a moment. "I thank God for the things I have, Micah. I thank God every day just for being alive." Cherish returned with huge towels in her hands and handed me one to dry off with.

I was still in awe of what I was seeing. I was walking around her room in my wet socks, amazed. "Yeah, whatever. Didn't you say you live with foster parents? That's like a job, ain't it? So they must get paid some kind of dough. Man, I need an application."

Cherish dried her long hair and then stomped her foot in frustration. "It's not about the money, Micah," she said. "These worldly things—these are all just borrowed things. Everything comes to an end. The Lord tells us to think not about the things we have, and to let him provide the things we need."

I dried my hair too with a towel. Not that I was copying her or anything, but I thought I shouldn't walk around with wet hair in her house. "Are you some kind of holy roller?" I asked.

Cherish laughed. "I'm almost afraid to ask, but what is a holy roller, Micah?"

I laughed too. "You know, someone who thinks they are Christian-perfect and devil-proof." I was still chuckling under my breath.

Cherish took off her socks and flung them into her laundry hamper. "No, I don't feel that way. Maybe one day I will explain things to you so you can better understand me, Micah. Until then, let's just get to know each other." Cherish flopped sideways across her big, pink canopy bed.

I flopped across her canopy bed too. Cherish bounced up a little and seemed startled by it. I began to bite my nails. "What do you mean, get to know each other?" I asked. "Look, Cherish, we can't be friends, because we will probably be enemies."

Cherish rolled over to one side, catching her head with her hand, looking puzzled. "Micah, I don't want to be your enemy, but I would like to be your friend."

I was confused why Cherish would want to be my friend. "Why?" I replied grudgingly. "I mean, you really don't even know me. I definitely don't know you."

Cherish let out a big sigh. "God tells us to love one another, regardless of the situation. I know you think I like Linwood, but that's just not true. I'm not interested in him at all."

"You're not? Oh, so you too good for my man, huh?" I asked.

"No, Micah, that's not what I mean," she replied in a stern voice. "Right now I have plenty of time to enjoy my youth. I'm not really interested in boys. I have too many other things on my mind."

"What other things, Cherish?" I asked. "You talk like an old woman. You don't sound like the rest of us. Are you from New York or something?"

Cherish got up from the bed and stood next to her bedroom window. I continued to lie on her bed. "No, Micah, it goes deeper than that. One day I will be glad to explain things to you, but not today. Today, the Holy Spirit tells me to befriend you, and I have to be obedient to the Holy Spirit, regardless of how ghetto you act!"

We both burst out laughing. I was beginning to feel more relaxed around Cherish. It was weird. In the short amount of time I'd known Cherish, I felt like I had known her all my life. Cherish had a kind of energy that made you drawn to her. I was so into our conversation that I didn't even notice the time.

I rolled over, catching a glance at Cherish's glass slipper-shaped clock. "Oh, my God, my grandma is going to kill me," I yelled. "Cherish, I'm late!"

I thanked Cherish for inviting me and dashed out the front door like Superman on steroids. I hopped on my bike and peddled like my life was depending on it—because it was. The only thing I could think about was Grandma Bean fussing me out. I knew she would probably assume that I had been out with Linwood kissing somewhere, but this time I hadn't been sneaky. I started crying, because I knew I was going to get a spanking when I got home.

Oh, Lord, I prayed, *please don't let me get in trouble. I promise, Lord, I won't be late again.* Every time I thought about Grandma Bean beating me, I thought about the time she caught me humping in my Girl Scout uniform. First she made me go upstairs and pick out a belt that she was going to spank me with. Then she chased me around the house. I was quick and could run fast. I slid under the bed like I was playing baseball and going for a homerun. My little hands grabbed hold of the box springs under the bed. Somehow I knew it was going to be a bumpy ride. Grandma Bean was so mad and so full of adrenaline that she'd picked up the whole bed; and when that bed flew up, I flew up with it, holding on like a baby kangaroo holding onto its mother!

I arrived at my house. I could see Grandma Bean cooking in the kitchen. I took a deep breath and opened up the front door. "Micah, hey baby, come here and give your Grandma Bean a kiss," she said.

I couldn't understand it. I mean, it looked like Grandma Bean, smelled like Grandma Bean, and acted like Grandma Bean—but was it really Grandma Bean?

Grandma Bean hugged me. "I ran into Ms. Robinson at the grocery store this afternoon, and she told me how you helped her new foster child Cherish in school today. She said Cherish told her how you introduced her to all your friends and even offered to walk her home, because she wasn't sure of the way. I told her that's how you are, always willing to help out somebody."

Cherish had saved me from a spanking! "Yeah, Grandma Bean, that's me—always ready to lend a helping hand," I said proudly. "You know, I think I'm going to go upstairs and do some homework right now. Bye, Grandma Bean, I'll see you later."

I quietly released a silent sigh and eased upstairs. I couldn't believe that Cherish had covered for me. I couldn't believe it because I'd been mean to her earlier that day. I couldn't wait to tell Shana about this news. I couldn't for the life of me figure out why Cherish had covered for me, but what I did know was that right now Grandma Bean thought I was a saint. Earlier, Cherish had mentioned that her family called her Cherry. I flopped open my math book to begin my homework and thought to myself, *I think I might give her a chance.*

Chapter Two

I couldn't wait to get to school the next day. Something inside me was so strong, I didn't even wait for Shana. I didn't quite know what it was. All I knew was that I needed to talk to Cherish. She had been on my mind all night. Somehow I didn't feel threatened by Cherish anymore. Maybe she was cool with me.

I rode my bike faster than ever before. I arrived at school and headed straight for my locker. Cherish's locker was one row down from mine, so we had to see each other. I tried to pretend like I was cool and had it going on as usual. Sure enough, there was Cherish closing her locker. She always looked like she had everything together. "Good morning, Micah," she said with a smile. "How are you today?"

I tried desperately to act cool, calm, and collected. I nodded my head as if to say *what's up* or *how are you.*

Cherish looked puzzled.

"What's up, Cherish," I said. "Let me holla at you for a second. Let's get something straight right now. I really appreciate what you did for me, but we need to keep this our little secret. You know, I gotta image around here to uphold. So just tell me what I owe you, and everything will be cool, okay?"

"Micah, you don't owe me anything," Cherish said. "A friend needed help, so I helped her. I didn't want you to get into trouble with your Grandma. I called Ms. Robinson before we left school. I always let her know what's going on."

Now I was puzzled. I didn't really understand my own feelings. First I'd been glad to see her; then I was interrogating her. "What do you mean you don't want anything?" I said. "Nothing in life is free, and besides, nobody does something for nothing. Don't tell me you did that out of the kindness of your heart, because you didn't. You want something from me, and you bet your bottom dollar I'm going to find out what it is."

Cherish smiled at me. "Micah, I don't want anything from you."

I opened my locker, threw my books in, and closed the door. "Looka here, missy," I replied angrily. "You'd just better tell me what you want from me, or it's on between you and me."

Cherish threw her books and closed her locker too. "Micah, I'm serious. You don't owe me anything. Do you always have a problem with people who try to help you out? Why are you so angry inside? Is there anything I can help you with?"

I started walking toward my classroom and then stopped to confront Cherish. "Why are you trying to be my friend? You don't even know me." I was screaming at her from the top of my lungs. "Haven't you learned yet? I haven't been nice to you since you stepped foot in this school. I have been nothing but mean to you. You think you know me, but you don't."

I began to cry. I began to cry real hard, almost like someone threw a ball in my stomach. I felt bad on the inside. For some reason, I began to think and reflect about my life, and I quickly grew angry toward her. Cherish was everything I wasn't. I supposed I carried a look on my face that told everyone I was going through something at home. People knew; they never had to ask me about my mother. I worried about the way I looked, because I didn't want to look, talk, or act like Mama. I had focused so much on growing up not following in her footsteps that somehow I'd lost myself.

Cherish reminded me of who I was. Granted, she never said so, but she was everything I wanted to be—normal, that is . . . a child enjoying life on life's terms. When I looked at Cherish, I saw a pretty girl enjoying life every day and loving everyone in it. So I hated her, because she was everything the devil had robbed from me. He'd taken away my joy, peace, and happiness.

I was so embarrassed, because I never cried in front of other people. Cherish looked at me. Without a word, she lifted up my chin and shook her head. She hovered over me as if she was protecting me from the people around us. We began to walk steadily and fast. I couldn't see anything, because my face was buried in Cherish's chest. The only thing I knew was that we were walking very fast.

After a while, I heard no more students—just birds and the sound of trees swaying in the wind. By the time I looked up, I didn't know where we were, exactly. We weren't in Kansas anymore, so to speak. I looked around at the beautiful scenery. The trees were very beautiful. We weren't far from the school, but I'd never know that place was even there.

"Cherish, where are we?" I asked. "What is this place. Are we skipping school?"

"This is my secret hiding place," she said. "There's a path that leads from the school to here. I like this big tree and the flowers that surround it. I like the dandelions here. Sometimes I come here just to get away from it all, and, yes, we are skipping for now. Even I have my breaking points. I like to sit under this big oak tree and just talk to God sometimes. It's like I can feel him listening to me, and I just want to be alone with him. Oh, I feel Jesus listening to me and healing me. Oh, forget it. You wouldn't understand." Cherish relaxed her head against the big oak tree.

I sat beside Cherish, wiping my tears. "Yes, I do," I told her. "Just because I'm not a holy roller, that doesn't mean I don't like to talk to God. Yeah, that's right, I talk to him. Yeah, we talk all the time. But you wouldn't understand that, with you being secretive and all."

Cherish had a puzzled look on her face. "What do you mean, I'm secretive?" she asked.

I walked over and pulled up a dandelion. I wanted to find out more about her. "Why you got to come all out here where the big oak tree is, huh? Could it be that you are ashamed to talk to God in the open? Yeah, maybe you ain't so holy after all. You just a little old holy secret.

By this time, I knew that I had struck a nerve with Cherry. If there was anything that would tick her off, it was talking about her God. I could see her face begin to turn red. Her eyebrows looked as if they were ready to take off. She got up from the tree and faced toward me like she really wasn't playing this time. "Look here, you old heathen!" she said, shaking her hand at my face.

No, she didn't! "Heathen!" I replied angrily. "No, you didn't just call me no heathen!"

"You got some nerve," Cherish shouted, "trying to tell me about my relationship with the Lord, when you the one don't halfway be paying attention in church. I guess you just like your mama—wild like a rose!" Suddenly she covered her mouth in embarrassment.

I couldn't say anything. I was speechless. But deep down, I knew it had been true. Maybe I *was* like my mama. I was her seed. I didn't say anything back to Cherish. I didn't feel like crying or fighting. At the moment, I just wanted to rest. I was tired, tired of being tired. I lay down in the hot grass. I forcefully grabbed a dandelion puff, like it was trying to escape from me. I took one big breath, and away the dandelion went. Up, up, and away. I watched it float into the air. It looked so free, and for one brief moment, I felt free too. I closed my eyes and made believe that the dandelion was me floating away from my problems.

"Micah, are you okay?" Cherish said, "'Cause I'm really sorry."

I sighed. "Cherish, dear, I'm sorry too," I replied.

"Micah, I know how it feels to be afraid of growing up to be like your parents."

"Oh, you don't know how it feels," I said. "You have everything. What more could you want?"

Cherish took a deep breath and then exhaled. "Simply to be loved. My mom and dad were atheist."

"Atheist? What does that mean?" I asked.

"It means you don't believe in anything, I guess," she replied.

"Oh, I see," I said.

Cherish grabbed a yellow dandelion and begin to pick at the flower. "I was about five years old when it all happened," she said. "I remember every day when my father went to work, this other man would come to the house. He didn't talk much. He would just pat me on my head, and then both him and my mother would go straight to the bedroom. They would stay in there for a long time.

"Well, this went on for a long time, until one day Daddy came home early, and the man was still there. Daddy sent me to my room. I heard a whole bunch of cussing and fussing. I even

25

heard some hitting and smacking. Then I heard a loud punch. I couldn't take it anymore, so I ran into their room. The man was bleeding badly. He was bleeding in his private area, but his private part was on the bed and his body wasn't. He just stood there screaming in pain, and Daddy stood in shock, holding a bloody knife. My mother called the police. The ambulance came to take the man to the hospital. He just kept hollering to my father, 'I'm going to kill you for doing this to me!'

"I was scared. My daddy went with the police, but he came back after a couple of days. They said it wasn't his fault, because it was his house, and that was self-defense. Things cooled down for a while, and I thought things were over. Then one night while we were eating dinner, a knock came at the front door. It was the same man. He looked furious. Daddy wouldn't move one inch, and he wasn't easily scared. Mama looked like she had seen a ghost. I had a terrible feeling in my stomach. The man pulled out a gun and shot my daddy, then my mommy, then shot at me, then himself."

"Wait a minute. Did you say the man shot at you?" I asked. "Where is your bullet wound?"

"Don't have one," she replied. "The bullet passed me and hit the wall instead. It was really close, though."

"Wow, that's impossible!" I was amazed by what Cherish had told me.

"All things are possible through Christ Jesus. As you can see, I survived. My first foster family was Christian, and that was new to me. Jesus really does save, Micah—literally! I must still be alive for some reason. I hope to bring people together. I had to learn to forgive my family, though. It was their careless actions that caused me to be without a family. Forgiveness is a powerful thing, Micah."

For some strange reason I really believed her. I knew she had to be telling the truth. I put my arm around Cherry. Somehow I really felt like she needed some love. She, in return, put her arm back around me. We just sat there in silence. There were no words.

As we stared at the sun going down, I realized our friendship was actually rising up. "Cherry?" I asked.

"Yeah?"

"Somehow I think we're going to be good friends."

Cherish smiled.

I overheard Grandma Bean crying on the phone the next morning. She was telling Mama to hold on and pray to the Lord about her situation. She just kept saying, "Hold on, baby, hold on." I bet Mama done got herself in trouble with the law again. The last time she was in jail, she promised to stop drinking, but sometimes I think she was prostituting too. Why didn't she just call Woody to get her out of jail? After all, he was her pimp/boyfriend.

I was tired of her always calling Grandma Bean and worrying her all the time. It just wasn't fair. And she was always asking me, "Micah why we don't ever talk anymore?" or "Why don't we act like mother and daughter?"

It's because you don't act like a mother, I thought. *If you acted like a mother, you'd get a daughter. Besides the fact that you are an alcoholic and probably the town prostitute, you're a lousy mom. Do you hear that, Ma? You're lousy!*

I felt myself getting angry. I'd promised myself that the woman wouldn't bother me anymore, but why was I letting her get to me again? I knew I needed to take my mind off her and watch a little TV.

Just when I was all set to watch my favorite show on television, Grandma Bean walked in the room. I knew by the look on her face that the news wasn't going to be good. I really didn't want to hear anything she had to say, especially if it had to do with Mama. Somehow my gut was telling me it did.

"Micah," she said, "turn the television off and come sit down by your grandma." She sat down on the bed. I could tell the news wouldn't be good.

"What is it, Grandma?" I asked reluctantly. "Everything okay?"

Grandma Bean let out a big sigh and replied, "It's about your mama. She's sort of in a bad situation right now, but she told me to tell you that she loves you and misses you a lot. Woody kind of messed her up really bad this time. She's in jail this week, but she'll be out before the weekend. She gave her life to Christ in jail. We talking now, and everything's real good between us. I've been praying about this to the Lord and—"

Oh, here we go again with Mama changing and all, I thought. My patience was so small when it came to Mama. "And *what,* Grandma Bean?"

Grandma Bean put her hand over her mouth and closed her eyes for a minute. Then she wiped a tear away. "And the Lord is telling me to forgive your mama of her past. She did give her life to Christ, and that means she deserves a second chance. I know you and your mama have some issues that you need to work out, but could you give her a second chance—for your grandma?"

"But Grandma Bean, she just ain't right!" I replied.

Grandma Bean was upset by my answer. "Now, Cakerbread, the Lord tells us to forgive. Can you be my good little Cakerbread and forgive your mama?"

I really didn't want to, but how could I disappoint Grandma Bean? "Yes, Grandma, I'll try," I replied.

Grandma Bean smiled and got up to walk to the door before stopping and turning back to look at me. "There's one more thing, honey. Sit back down. I need to discuss this with you. I'm going to go out of town this weekend to get some test done with my blood."

My heart sank to the floor. "What's wrong, Grandma Bean? What's wrong with your blood?"

I knew there was something else Grandma Bean had been holding out on me. If she told me she was sick, why, I didn't know what I would do. My Grandma Bean may have gossiped too much, and sure, she made me go to church every Sunday and made me serve on the usher board—but she was the sweetest woman I knew.

Grandma Bean had raised me ever since I was a newborn Cakerbread. And she'd called me Cakerbread for as long as I could remember. She said she used to bake it when I was a baby, and I'd just loved to eat it. She was the only mother I'd ever known. Grandma Bean would probably be the *only* mother I would ever know. *Please, Lord,* I prayed. *Don't be so cruel as to take my Grandma Bean away from me. Don't take the very reason for my breathing. I don't want to live without her. When she lives, I live. If she dies, I die.*

Grandma Bean rushed back to hug me. "Now, baby, it's just blood test. I'm fine. While I'm away this weekend, I thought it would be a good idea for your mother to stay with you. Y'all can talk and go to church together. You can even show off that new uniform I bought you for ushering. Now wouldn't that be nice?"

"No!" I replied in a stern voice. I did not want to be left with that woman!

"What if I said you could invite your friends over and have a sleepover?" Grandma asked. "That way they could get to know your mom. Yeah, Micah, let them be introduced to the new, clean and sober, Christian Irish. Now wouldn't that be something to be proud of?" Grandma Bean anxiously awaited my answer.

Who was I kidding? I couldn't hurt Grandma Bean's feelings. "Well," I said, "I guess so, Grandma Bean. If you think it's a good idea, then I would be willing to give her a second chance."

"Now that's my Cakerbread," she said. "Give Grandma Bean a big hug."

As I hugged Grandma, I couldn't help thinking to myself about all the fun I was going to have that weekend. It was going to be the best weekend ever! I couldn't wait to call Shana and Cherry. We could have fun all night. We could even stay up late! Mama probably wouldn't care anyway. I should have felt guilty for thinking that way, but I didn't. I felt like it was payback time!

I couldn't wait to talk to Cherish that morning at school. I waited by her locker, but I didn't see her. I spotted Shana at the water fountain, sipping, as usual. "What's up, Shana?" I said to her.

Shana did not look happy. "Why you ain't called me in a while, Micah?"

The truth was, Cherish and I were becoming best friends, and I hadn't wanted to hurt Shana's feelings. Shana was still my friend, and we would always be friends, for that matter.

"I don't know," I said. "I just been busy and stuff. But hey, you want to come over to my house for a sleepover this weekend? My Grandma Bean is going out of town, and she said I could have a sleepover while she's away. Oh, my God, you have to say yes. We are going to have so much fun this weekend. I just can't wait!"

Shana paused for a second and took her lip gloss out of her purse and attempted to reapply it to her lips. "Well, it does sound like fun, but I have a dance recital this weekend. My mom is looking forward to it, so you know I can't miss it. Who else have you invited?" she asked.

I was hesitant about telling her I wanted to invite Cherish. "Well, I was about to ask Cherish, whenever she brings her slow butt to school."

Shana dropped her lip gloss on the floor. "Did you just say *Cherry*?" she asked.

I stooped down to pick her lip gloss and handed it back to her as a peaceful gesture. "Man, don't trip, Shana," I replied. "She's cool. We've been hanging out together. It's just we have a lot in common. You should really get to know her a little better. You really shouldn't be so closed-minded, Shana. You could be missing out on meeting new people like that."

Shana almost knocked the lip gloss out of my hand, she was so angry. "Me, miss out on meeting new people?" she said in an angry voice. "*You* were the one jealous of her."

I tried to play it off. "Me, jealous? Please, girl, I was just testing her to see if she could be one of the crew. She passed with flying colors!"

"Yeah, right. In other words, you couldn't find anything to hate about her, so you had no choice but to like her."

I always hated when Shana was right, and she always loved it. Even when we were babies, she just had to prove her point that we could only pee-pee *in* the potty and not *on* it. "Shana, Shana, Shana. What am I going to do with you?"

Shana snatched her lip gloss out of my hand. "Let's just go to class, please. Yeah, you know I'm right, Micah. When are you going to appreciate me?"

"Man, don't you have some news you should be reporting?" I asked.

She always hated when I referred to her nosiness. That would teach her to rub my nose into my own mistakes!

Cherish and I had been meeting regularly after school at the big oak tree. It had come to be our secret place. Nobody knew about it—not even Shana. We didn't tell Shana for good reason, of course. If we told her, then she would broadcast it all over school, and then everyone would be hiding out there instead of going to class. Cherish and I still hung out with Shana, though, and sometimes with Linwood too, when he wasn't acting a fool and getting into fights with other boys. It was a rare occasion when he wasn't fighting somebody. He was really beginning to get on my nerves.

Sometimes Cherish would bring the Bible, and we would read it out loud. Pastor Jacobs told me I was doing much better when called upon to recite my Bible verses in Sunday school. Cherish and I just looked at each other and smiled. Nobody knew. I think Grandma Bean did, though, because she always asked Cherish to sit beside us. Sometimes she would pick Cherish up for church in the morning.

I could not wait to meet with Cherish after school one day to see what she'd brought. We were always bringing things to show and tell about, like were in kindergarten or something. "Did you bring it?" I asked her, barely keeping my excitement under control.

"Bring what?" she asked.

"Don't hold out on me, Cherish," I replied, even more excited. "I've been waiting to see it all day!"

Cherish giggled under her breath. "I have no earthly idea what you are talking about."

I couldn't take it anymore. I needed to know if she'd brought it. "If you don't let me see it, I won't be your friend," I said.

"Okay, okay, close your eyes and I'll hand it to ya," she replied.

I closed my eyes and opened my hands. Cherry laid the object in my hands and then instructed me to open my eyes. There it was! I had never seen anything like it before. It felt kind of funny. Sure, Grandma had one, but not like this. This one was different. It had class, style, and look at the color!

"Behold, Micah, I give you the ultimate training bra!" she shouted, surprising me.

Wow, it really was one. "Can I keep it?" I asked. "I love it!"

Cherish grabbed the training bra back from my hand. "What for? You don't need it yet." Cherish laughed.

"I know you ain't talking, Cherish," I replied. "You the same size I am, so don't trip."

Cherish let out a sigh. "Well, I guess you can have it. Consider this a friendship present."

"Friends?" I said. "I consider us sisters."

I knew this was a touchy subject, one that we had not discussed. I didn't have any sisters or brothers, so occasionally I felt lonely.

Cherish threw her arm around me and pretended to put me in a headlock. "Micah, I really like you. You're my best friend. I want us to be more than sisters, but it's too bad you're going to hell."

I dropped my books and stood up, placing my hand on my hip with an attitude. "Hey, that's not nice!" I shouted.

Cherish ran her fingers through her long hair and then replied, "But it's true, Micah. You're not saved. Sure, you attend church, and you're on the usher board, but you haven't given your life to Jesus Christ."

I sat in silence for a moment. Deep down, I knew she was right. I didn't want to go to hell. I wanted to go to heaven with everybody else. Most importantly, I wanted to see Jesus. I didn't want to see the devil. And I never wanted me and Cherish to part. "What must I do to be saved?" I asked.

Cherish opened up her Bible and went to work, and under that very same oak tree, I got saved! After that, I seemed to change all over. I mean, I was still the same age, but I felt different, talked different, and even smelled different. Cherish told me, no matter what, to always trust in the Lord. The next day we talked with Pastor Jacobs, and he baptized me. He told me that was the best decision anyone could ever make. Yep, that was the beginning of a new life.

When Friday night arrived, my mom came home, and Grandma Bean left town as soon as Mama arrived. Mama and I were strangers in the house. We didn't talk at all. We had nothing to talk about. She didn't know me, and I didn't know her. While I was waiting for Cherish to arrive, I picked out several movies for us to watch. That way she wouldn't have time to ask questions about my mama.

Surprise, surprise. Woody showed up that night. If Grandma Bean had known he was there, she would have had a fit! I peeked around the corner so I could see what Woody and Mama was up to. They lay all on the couch, kissing and hugging on each other. Looked like a bear and a deer in heat. They made me so sick. I couldn't wait till Grandma Bean got back.

Someone was knocking at the door, and I suspected it was Cherish. She always arrived on time. I was glad to see her. We immediately went upstairs to my room, popped in the movies, and watched them one by one. Pretty soon it was bedtime. She never asked me about Woody and Mama. Somehow, I believe she already knew.

Woody entered the room and told us he'd made a goodnight drink for us downstairs. Somehow I didn't trust it, but Cherish said we shouldn't be rude and should at least drink it and then go to bed. As we passed by Grandma Bean's bedroom, I could see Mama lying drunk on the bed, curled up with a bottle of Wild Irish Rose. She was supposed to be changed? Yeah right!

In the kitchen, I was beginning to feel a little bit nervous. I could see Woody out of the corner of my eye, staring at Cherish's body. He disgusted me! Woody handed us the drinks and told us to drink it all up. We did exactly what he said. He had the most devilish smirk on his face. Soon his smirk began to turn into fuzziness—then, complete darkness.

I didn't know what had happened to me. I couldn't move, I was so weak. I heard voices calling my name. "Micah, Micah," they said. "Help me! Help!" But I couldn't move. I couldn't do anything but lie there, paralyzed by the devil.

After a while, my eyes began to open. The sunlight hurt my eyes. I rubbed them because they felt so sore. My head hurt. It felt like someone had beaten me up or something. I slowly lifted myself to the kitchen counter. The two glasses were there, but no Cherish. I couldn't believe it was morning. What had happened to the night? I felt something sticky and wet on my hands. As soon as my eyes hit my nightgown, I was speechless. It was blood! Was I hurt? Did my period start? I checked my panties and looked at myself in the mirror. It wasn't me.

Oh, my God, something had happened last night. I ran through the house looking for Cherish. Mama was gone. Woody was gone too. Something inside told me to stop running and look inside my bedroom. I slowly opened my bedroom door. I was speechless. No words could come out of my mouth because of what I saw.

There was Cherish. Her arms were folded inward. My bedspread that had once been white was now red from her blood. Her eyes were still open. I tiptoed closer to her. I still could not speak. It felt like something was directing me to her body. I knew she was dead. Silently, I called her name. Then I whispered, "Cherish.

Cherish, can you hear me?" There was no answer. Something set me loose. I ran as fast as I could outside and screamed out, "Jesus, help me!" and collapsed in the front yard. There were no more words, no more nothing.

"Micah, can you hear me? Micah, baby, it's me, Grandma Bean."

I opened my eyes and flung myself into Grandma Bean's arms. I began to cry. Grandma Bean comforted me and told me everything was going to be all right. For just one moment I felt safe.

"Grandma Bean, what happened?" I asked. "Where am I?"

"Micah, I don't know how to tell you this." Grandma began to cry. I already knew Cherish was dead. Half of me felt dead. Grandma Bean had merely confirmed my thoughts. She told me the police said our drinks had been drugged. She said the medical evaluation confirmed that Cherish had been raped while we were unconscious. I never woke up, but Cherish did. The rumor was that Mama said Woody told her he had to kill Cherish, or he would go to jail. He didn't want any witnesses. He'd slit her throat, and in the morning, I'd found her dead.

Grandma Bean said I'd gone into shock and sort of lost my mind for a while. She told me I had been in the hospital for three months. The doctors said I didn't even know my name. How had all this happened without me even knowing it? How had I missed Cherish's funeral? Why had it happened?

Grandma Bean said Woody had talked Mama into pleading guilty to murdering Cherish. He promised her he would get her out somehow, but there was no need in him going to jail if he didn't have a criminal record. Besides, Woody had used a condom, so nothing linked him to the crime. Grandma Bean said Mama got life in prison. She said Mama loved Woody and would have done anything for him, even if it meant dying in prison.

Chapter Three

It was a few days after I'd come back home. Grandma Bean never did tell me her test results. I guess I sort of blocked that out of my mind. I hadn't been back to school. Shana has been calling me, but I just told Grandma Bean to tell her I was tired. Pastor Jacobs came by every day to check on me. He told me they missed me on the usher board. I told him I missed Cherish.

I just didn't understand why Jesus hadn't helped her like he had before. I barely read the Bible anymore. I couldn't even remember the last time I'd gone to church. I was angry because Cherish was gone, and I didn't understand why I was still there. I remembered what Cherish said about always trusting in the Lord, no matter what. *Where are you God?* I asked God. *Did you forget me?* Days came, and days went, but for me, life just seemed to stand still.

By the springtime of my seventh-grade year, I had missed so many days of school, it became necessary for me to attend summer school. Grandma Bean begged me to go. In many ways, Grandma Bean didn't want me to end up like my wild mama. There was nothing in the world I wouldn't do for Grandma Bean, even if it meant getting myself together and going to school. One thing for sure about black folks, if there is some good gossip going on, you had better believe the whole town is aware of it. Everywhere I looked, some kid or somebody was talking about me. Somebody told Grandma Bean I was crazy as a bat! I even heard one woman tell my Grandma Bean she could get a check for me from the government because my mind wasn't right no more. I never seen Grandma Bean get so mad she showed her color—till that day.

The first day of summer school arrived, and I was nervous as a rabbit! I really didn't want to go. Grandma Bean always told me to read Psalm 37 and not pay any of the children any attention. She dropped me off at school and sped off into the sunlight. I had begged her to let me miss the first day, but Grandma wouldn't hear of it. She handed me the small version of the King James Bible and practically pushed me out of the car. I took a deep breath and closed the door, blowing a good-bye kiss to her.

My feet felt like a pot of heavy bricks every time I took a step toward the entrance of the school. The sunlight was beaming so hard, I had to cover part of my face to shield me from the sunlight. Grandma Bean always said she didn't want no purple kids.

As I walked toward the entrance, there on the stairs stood a beautiful little girl with long red hair. I walked closer to her, and my feet certainly became lighter. The girl motioned her hand to come closer, and I did. It was Cherish! I could see her lips forming the words, "Come on, you can do it, Micah." I started running toward her, yelling, "Don't leave me again!" Cherish ran toward me, catching me by the arm. I was so tired, I tripped and fell to the ground. Cherish reached out her hand as if she wanted to help me up.

I took her hand gladly and allowed her to pull me up on my feet. "Cherish!" I yelled. "I thought you were dead!"

"Micah, it's me, Shana, your best friend, remember?" Shana said.

I was confused for a moment, but it was indeed Shana. I was just having a difficult time living in reality. "But I thought you were Cherish." The sadness overflowed my voice. I fought back the tears. Shana knew I was still hurting.

"I just came by to wish you a good start in summer school," Shana said. "Your grandma told me you would be starting today, and since I was doing my paper route on this block, it seemed like a good idea to see you off to school. I really haven't heard much from you, Micah. Ever since the, um . . . you know . . . incident, you just sort of disappeared, I guess. Even Linwood told me he hadn't seen you. Boy, Micah, I never thought you would ditch Linwood."

"Did you say *paper route?*" I asked. "When did you take up an interest in working?"

Shana flipped through some newspapers to see if they were in order. "Come on, Micah. Stop trying to change the subject. I know Cherish's death was hard, but it was hard on all of us. Do you know how guilty I felt for not coming over that night? I should have been there for you. I knew you didn't have a good relationship with your mother, but I never knew she was capable of killing someone."

"You don't know what you're talking about, Shana!" I told her.

Shana looked puzzled. "Micah, one day you just gonna have to face the truth," she said.

I was furious. "Shana, shut up!" I yelled.

"Why are you mad at me? I'm not the one who killed Cherish!"

"And what makes you think my mother killed Cherish?" Shana just stood there like I was a mental patient, dealing with major issues. I knew the whole town thought my mother had killed Cherish. Even long after the funeral, I hadn't talked with anyone. Why would I talk to them people? They all had their opinion of what had happened anyway. Besides, my town loved gossip, and if Mama didn't kill Cherish, there would be no gossip. The sad thing was, everyone knew Woody was capable of killing someone. Everyone was just too afraid of him to say it out loud.

"Micah, I never meant to upset you this morning. You have to believe it was not my intention to hurt you. Honestly, Micah, I really miss you. I just want my friend back, ya know?"

"Shana I know you would never do anything to hurt me on purpose. There are some things I'm dealing with on the inside right now. Just believe that I am not crazy like everyone says I am. Hey, you know what? Why don't I call you tonight to let you know what happened today in school?"

Shana appeared relieved. "That's my girl. Look, call me as soon as you get home. Please, don't let me have to call you first. See you later, Micah."

Shana waved good-bye and headed off to finish the rest of her route. I was proud of Shana for doing something this summer besides spending all of her parents' money. Suddenly I realized Shana was really and truly a good friend. Shana and I would always be friends until the day we died. Only, at that moment, I didn't like to think about death at all. I wondered what Linwood was up to. Part of me really missed him. I had pushed so many people away from me since Cherish's death that no one bothered to embrace me anymore, including Linwood. Boy, that hurt just to think about it.

I took a deep breath and proceeded down the hall to my first class. Of course, I found it necessary to find a seat in the back.

That way I figured the teacher would at least have to call on several people she could see, rather than little old me. Plus, I was a certified loner. If anyone wanted to talk to me or be my new friend, I wouldn't allow them to. I was too dangerous of a person, according to the rumors about me. I twirled my hair and wisped my bangs out of my eyesight.

The bell rang, and the other kids began to enter the classroom. Some of them looked at me, and some of them didn't. I smiled, faking it as much as possible.

The teacher walked in and set her books down on the desk. "Good morning, class. My name is Mrs. Thomas. I am going to be your math teacher for this summer. Why don't we all stand up and introduce ourselves?"

Oh, great. Why did we have to get personal so soon? I hated introducing myself. People stared all in my face. I really didn't have much to say besides my name, and she couldn't make me!

One by one, the kids introduced themselves. I started to fall into a daze. They were taking so long, talking about themselves. One girl stated how she was a model, and another boy talked about how he'd got a brand new BB gun that summer. Pretty soon I started to feel myself dozing off.

Someone whispered in my ear. "Psst. You're next, Micah," the voice said.

I felt someone shoving my arm. I opened my eyes to a pretty, dark-skinned girl with shoulder-length, curly hair. Her smile was warm and friendly. She was sort of overweight—not that I had noticed or anything, but you could tell she had certainly put away some biscuits in her days. She was a chocolate girl with pretty, smooth skin.

"Micah, you're next." The teacher motioned me to stand up and introduce myself.

"Well, uh, uh, my name is Micah, and that's all that I got to say. Thank you." I quickly sat back down.

Mrs. Thomas looked at me with discontent, as if I was holding something back. I could tell she wanted me to go on. "Well, Micah, is there anything else you want to tell us about yourself at all?" she asked.

I felt the overweight girl staring at me. She was all in my business, staring at me so hard she could count the hairs in my nose!

I cleared my throat before replying, "No, Mrs. Thomas, I don't have anything else to say right now."

I heard one of the boys snicker and whisper under his breath, "Yeah, her mama's a killer, heh, heh."

I rolled my eyes toward him so fast, I could have cut off his head!

Mrs. Thomas took the ruler and whacked the desk hard. "Settle down, class," she said in a stern voice. "We have a lot to cover over the summer."

The big girl leaned over and whispered to me. "Don't pay them fools any attention. They just trying to figure you out, girl. Now, you and I gonna have to exchange phone numbers. I can't afford to fail this class in summer school. Then everyone gonna know I'm dumb as a bat! So, what do ya say, Micah?" she asked.

I turned around slowly so I could address her properly. "Excuse you, and what is your name?" I was amazed this girl was acting like she knew me or something. I folded my arms and leaned toward her as if I was demanding an answer.

She leaned back into me and replied, "Oh, I guess you wasn't listening when I introduced myself to the class. My name is Brandy. Brandy Lane."

Brandy leaned toward me with a smirk on her face and then held out her hand to greet mine. Brandy insisted we exchange numbers. At that point, I really didn't care. I took out a piece of paper and wrote my number down for her. Brandy'd had her number ready for me before even asking.

After school, I waited for Grandma Bean to pick me. I didn't want Brandy to see me, but she did anyway. She went out of her way to wave to me before getting in her car and yelled, "Bye, girl, I'll see ya tomorrow."

I waved bye to Brandy just as Grandma Bean pulled up, all the while whispering under my breath, "Damn, she saw me."

I quickly got into the car and let out a big sigh, not realizing Grandma Bean might have heard me. She looked at me as if I was crazy and said, "Did you just curse, girl?"

Oh, I just couldn't afford to get into trouble that day and replied, "No, Grandma, I didn't say nothing . . . nothing at all."

She pressed the accelerator and started to drive off. "Well, it seems like you making friends already, girl. I knew your first day would go well. Did you read the Scripture I told you to read?" she asked.

"Yeah, Grandma, I read it just like you told me to," I replied. I hadn't really read it, but if Grandma thought it made a difference, then I'd give her that."

"And because you read it, that made a big difference in your day, didn't it?" Grandma Bean smiled.

I let out a big sigh and replied, "Yeah, Grandma Bean, it made my day better." I turned and looked at her. I knew she was enjoying this moment. She always took pleasure out of thinking God done something. She didn't care what it was, long as she thought God did it. She drove away from the school, smiling ear to ear. It looked like somebody'd super-glued her lips from one ear to the other.

"See, look at God, girl!" she yelled excitedly.

That night, Grandma Bean made biscuits, country fried steak, rice, and butter beans with iced tea. She said a woman needs a good meal as much as a man. I took the last piece of biscuit and swirled it around in the gravy on my plate. Grandma Bean sure could cook. I thought to myself and wondered if I would be a good mama like my grandma some day. I wondered how could my own mama turn out so bad?

Sometimes Grandma overlooked the bad things Mama did. That made me angry. I remember one time Mama had stolen some money from Grandma. I know it hurt her real bad. I heard her crying about it and talking with Pastor Jacobs. Whenever she confronted Mama, Mama would yell that it was Grandma's fault she was the way she was. Mama said Grandma should have trusted her. Grandma wouldn't talk to me about it, so I didn't ask.

Grandma Bean went to the jail to see Mama every visiting day and stayed for the whole visiting hour. She brought Mama cigarettes and whatever else she asked for. Grandma went up to that prison faithfully, just like she went to church. Sometimes I would try to keep her from going to see Mama by pretending to be sick. She would just shake her head and tell me I had better make peace with the bitterness in my heart for Mama. She always said the devil was feeding off of it. Nevertheless, Mama had done a horrible thing to me. She had chosen Woody over me and Cherish. In my book, she needed to rot in that prison!

The phone rang and Grandma Bean answered. "Micah, telephone," she said and handed it to me.

I wasn't expecting any calls. "Hello."

"Hey, I just called to see how you were doing," a voice said.

"Who is this?" I asked.

"Linwood, your boy! What, you forgot about me?"

Whenever Linwood was nervous, he always had to put some kind of emphasis on himself. My stomach felt like butterflies were roaming around in it. I had missed Linwood. I thought he had joined every other kid in town and hated me. It had become easier for me to avoid everyone rather than to talk about what had happened to Cherish.

"No, I haven't forgotten you. What you been up to?" I asked.

"Nothing much. Dad got me going to church now with him. Dad said since I ain't working nowhere, I could at least give the Lord some time. You know how Mr. McDaniel is. He gonna make sure I'm doing something round here. It sho is too hot to work outside. The south stay hot during the summer time. I ain't working on nobody's tobacco field this year. Besides, this is the first summer I ain't went to summer school. I actually think he's proud of me, Micah."

Linwood's dad could sing his tail off. I almost forgot how good he sang on Sundays. Poor Linwood, having to go back to church. After his mama died, he told me he wouldn't ever attend church again. He said God needed to come to him, and not him come to God. I was surprised, because Linwood's mother had stayed in church. That was really when he had started being bad and stuff. He'd never been in that much trouble when his mother was living.

46

Now he was always smoking somebody's marijuana somewhere. One time he even grew his own in science class. Linwood told the teacher it had healing power. Of course, he got suspended and almost went to jail. Everybody just sort of felt sorry for him because he'd lost his mother. Now Mr. Jenkins was raising the boy on his own. That in itself was a full-time job.

"Shana told me she saw you at school," he said.

"Oh, yeah? Well, what did she say?" I was afraid of what Shana might have told him, like I was going crazy or something. After all, I had called her Cherish.

"She said you looked real good and was doing well," he replied.

For once, Shana had kept her big mouth shut. Maybe she had just felt so sorry for me that she didn't want anyone to know. Oh, well. I was just glad she hadn't told Linwood.

"So, you want to get together tomorrow night?" he asked. "We could go to a matinee at the movies. You know, I'm fifteen now."

"And?"

"And that means we could see a PG-13 movie. So what time shall I pick you up?" In the south, nobody cared if you drove at fifteen. I mean, what were you gonna hit, a deer or something? Kids round there drove tractor trailers at fourteen!

Then I thought, *How dare he, always thinking I want to see him? He think he all that!* But who was I kidding? I always had a funny feeling it was going to be something special between Linwood and me. "Come to my house about noon," I said.

"All right. Peace, Micah."

Why couldn't he just say good-bye like other normal black men?

"Peace," I replied.

Linwood arrived on time and with company. There was Shana staring at me with those big old brown eyes of hers. She could look at you, and her eyes would do all the communicating. Linwood never seemed to mind, though, when Shana would invite herself to places she had no business going. The funny thing was, she would act like she was supposed to be there.

"As you can see, I have company." Linwood pointed to Shana with a smirk on his face. He knew I was looking forward to spending time with him and him only. Shana folded her arms and pooched out what little tail she had. She gave him that ghetto, what-you-trying-to-say look.

Shana rolled her eyes. "Anyway, Micah girl, I knew you wasn't going to see a scary movie without me."

Shana waited for a response. Her body posture was really saying, *How come you hanging out with Linwood and not me?*

"Uh, Shana, ya know I was going to call you about that," I answered. "The funny thing is, you found out before I could ask you, ya know, with you being Channel 2 News and all."

Linwood interrupted and stated, "Micah, I told Shana we were going to the movies."

"Oh, I knew that," I replied. I gave him the most threatening look. He lifted his hands like he had no control over the situation. He knew I was going to cuss him out after the movie.

"Well, let's go," I said. "I got other things to do when I get home."

"Micah," Shana said, "what do you have to do other than ditch your best friend for a man?"

I gave Shana the hand, snatched Linwood's arm, and proceeded toward the car. Shana's mouth dropped wide open. I could tell she was angry. She stomped her feet and headed toward the car. She flopped down in the backseat of the car and then slammed the door.

"Hey, girl," Linwood yelled, "this car ain't paid for yet!"

I could tell it had really made Linwood mad, because he floored that little '87 Escort right out of the driveway!

Chapter Four

After the movies, Linwood and I dropped Shana off and spent the whole day together. I must admit, it felt like old times again. We had a good time together. How could I forget how much he made me laugh? Of course, he looked like a typical gangster, but deep down inside, I knew he had a heart. I also knew he really liked me, perhaps even loved me. Or maybe he was just used to being with me. After all, I had been with Linwood off and on since elementary school. Ever since that first day of kindergarten when he'd punched out Sammy, the white boy who sat beside me in class, I knew it was love.

Linwood stood by his word of having God come to him. Every Sunday during the altar call, Linwood would get up and walk out the door. The ushers would ask him to stay for the altar call, but Linwood would just walk right past them, not even looking back. Mr. McDaniel always had a sad face when Linwood walked out. Sometimes Mr. McDaniel even cried, like it hurt him so much or something. Maybe he thought Linwood was a lost cause or something. I don't know. Linwood was a lot to handle, even for me!

Shana and I had developed a routine. She fussed me out for spending time with Linwood and not her. I tell ya, there is not enough of me to go around these days. I walked to summer school with Shana; that way she could do her paper route while we gossiped on the latest issues. There I'd be, running beside

Shana while she was throwing out newspapers—tearing up people's lawns, of course. If it rained, Grandma Bean would take us on the paper route and me to school. Shana and I would go on and on, gossiping in the back of the car, almost missing some people's houses. Of course, you know Channel 2 knew everything and anything that was going on.

As we were riding our bikes one morning, Shana brought up Brandy Lane. "So you wanna know about Ms. Brandy Lane. Huh, huh, don't ya?" she asked me.

"I'm almost afraid to ask what you know, girl," I replied.

"Well, since you got it out of me. Brandy lives with her aunt, who may very well be her mother, who she thinks her sister is her sister, but may be her real mother. Micah, are you following what I am saying?"

By that time, I had a blank look on my face. Shana knew she had lost me somewhere between the first and last sentence. "You have got to be making this up," I said.

Shana looked offended. "I'm not," she said. "I got it from some very reliable sources. Only I can't reveal my sources to you."

"Shana you had better tell me, or else," I said in a stern voice.

"Or else what? I can't help it if I have more pull than you do!"

I gave Shana the meanest look ever. At that point, she had me so intrigued about the girl that I had to know if it was real or not.

Shana covered her mouth as if to try to keep the information captive in her mouth. Then she blurted out, "Okay, since you my girl, I'll tell you!"

Shana leaned off her bike toward me, then lifted back up to see who was standing around, then leaned again toward my ear and whispered, "The old ladies who do the church bulletin told me. See? I told you it was reliable information!"

I took off running toward school. I knew if God was listening to Shana, she would surely be struck by lightning!

Shana was obviously insulted and shouted, "Hey, girl, don't you tell nobody what I told you. That's classified information!" She turned her bike around and proceeded with her paper route.

By that time, I was in the building, safe and sound. I slowly walked into the classroom and plopped into my chair. I couldn't believe what kind of day I was having already. What else could happen?

I guess I spoke too soon, because there came Brandy, walking in like she owned everything. Brandy was chewing gum so hard I could hear her smacking. Brandy waved at me as she made her way into the class. *Oh, Lord, please don't let her sit by me!*

Brandy sat down next to me and whispered, "Hey, girl, what's up?"

"Hey, how are you?" I replied, just trying to be polite.

I really didn't want to say anything to her at that point. I mean, who invited her to sit by me, anyway?

"Did you do your homework?" she asked. "I had a little trouble with my homework. We really must get together soon, okay?"

"Yeah, sure," I said.

Just as Brandy was about to start a conversation with me, in came a tall white man with a whole lot of books. He was sort of slim, so I knew he had to be struggling with them. Suddenly one of the books teetered off the stack. I jumped up to catch the book before it fell.

"Thanks, little lady," he said. "I almost lost one!"

"No problem, sir," I replied.

He laughed. "Please, don't call me *sir*. I'm not that old yet. By the way, good morning, class. I will be your new teacher. Mrs. Thomas is no longer with the school system, so I will be taking over for the rest of the summer."

You could hear the whispering spread like wildfire. I could hear some children say, "I bet she finally got caught with Mr. Eagle (the school janitor)." I tell you, when I grow up, I don't want to be stuck in this town. These people are ready for you to fail!

The teacher cleared his throat and said, "Why don't we start out by introducing ourselves. My name is Alex Tillman. I just graduated from college with a degree in mathematics. I just got married finally, and I am very excited to start teaching."

I asked, "Uh, Mr. Tillman, could you tell me what happened to Mrs. Thomas?"

Mr. Tillman paused with a blank look on his face. I know he was probably thinking, *Who is this little black girl asking me about her old teacher?*

"Well, Mrs. Thomas decided she wanted to be a stay-at-home mom," he replied.

I sat back and smiled, looking around the classroom. Well, I bet that shut all those little gossipers up real quick!

Mr. Tillman cleared his throat and said, "Why don't you start first with the introductions. Class be careful that you hear everyone's name, because I am going to pair you up as homework buddies. You will be responsible for doing a number of assignments together—not all of them, but a majority of them. I feel it is important to learn together. That way we will all be on the same page."

Somehow I felt as if Mr. Tillman had put me on the spot. I really don't like interacting with other people besides Shana and Linwood. I tried with others before, and look what happened to Cherish. I don't even like introducing myself to other people. I don't know them, and they don't know me. Nevertheless, I went ahead and introduced myself as instructed by Mr. Tillman. It was going to be a long day.

Grandma Bean came to pick me up from school on time as usual. Grandma Bean had a whole big bushel of field peas in the back of the car. I knew this was a bad sign—all those field peas and only one grandchild!

"Micah, when you get home, I got a big surprise for you!" she said excitedly.

"Does it involve field peas?" I asked.

"No, but you will be shulling them!" she replied.

"Grandma Bean, that ain't fair! Most kids don't have to shull peas! My fingers are gonna be real stinking!"

She gave me a real serious look. "Never mind the peas, girl. Just wait till we get home, and you won't be thinking about those peas!" She smiled at me, giving me her "it's okay" look. I didn't know what she had in store for me, but I sure hoped it didn't involve shulling those peas!

As soon as we arrived at home, Grandma Bean hurried me out of the car and into the house. I opened the front door and, to my surprise, there were a big bouquet of flowers and balloons. It wasn't my birthday or anything, so I couldn't figure out why I would receive all those flowers and balloons. My mouth dropped open with surprise. I walked over to the flowers and picked out the card attached to them. The card read, "I hope one day you will come to forgive me. Love, your Mama."

Grandma Bean was excited and said, "I bet you wasn't thinking your mama would send you something like that in the mail, now, did you? I tell you, Micah, I think your mama has learned her lesson in that jail she's in. The poor girl shouldn't be in jail anyway."

I took the card and ripped it up and yelled, "Yes, she should!" I shouted to the top of my voice. Suddenly I drew up a fist and punched one of the balloons. Then I grabbed the whole vase of flowers and flung them to the ground, breaking the whole vase.

Grandma Bean stood back as if the crash had startled her. "Child, what has gotten into you?" she asked.

I started to cry. I couldn't believe that woman had the nerve to send me flowers and apologize! There was no amount of apologizing in this world that would make up for Cherish's death! In my eyes, she was just as guilty as Woody was. In my opinion, Irish chose Woody over me when she took the rap for him. All I could think about was her suffering in that jail.

Grandma Bean grabbed my arm and said, "Now you listen to me, Micah. Holding a grudge against your poor mama ain't doing nothing but giving the devil room to dwell on the inside of ya. If you truly want to be set free, you gonna have to forgive your mama. The Bible says to honor thy mother and thy father. Now, like it or not, there ain't no exceptions to the rule!"

I folded my arms on the inside of me and flung my body against the wall. Suddenly I felt myself sliding against the wall and coming down until I hit the floor. I began to sob and cry. It wasn't my normal trying-to-be-cute cry. I cried like a baby—with no pride, no shame, and a roller coaster of emotions. Grandma Bean walked over, reached down, and put her arms around me.

What a predicament Grandma Bean must have been in to have her grandchild hate *her* own child so much. "I know this is hard on you," she said, "and it is also hard on me. I don't know why your mother did so many things to you. Your mother isn't the only one to blame. I did my share of dirt too. That's probably why your mama turned out the way she did."

"Stop making excuses for her!" I shouted. "You are always making excuses for her!"

"Micah, the important thing you need to be concentrating on is getting yourself right with God. No, your mother didn't take your side. And yes, she did go through the same exact experience, but she is accountable for herself. When you are standing in line with God, you are standing in line with everything that you are accountable for. Baby, as long as I have been saved, I know you cannot find peace with unforgiveness in your heart. Honey, I am warning you to let this go!"

I stumbled up the stairs and into my bedroom, leaving Grandma Bean at the bottom of the stairs. So much had happened that my brain went into information overload. I just wanted rest for a few minutes. I grabbed Willy, my teddy bear, and dozed off to sleep, hoping to put this day behind me.

Chapter Five

"Micah, telephone!" Grandma Bean yelled.

I must have been asleep for a long time, because I could hear Grandma downstairs frying some fish. I hoped it was flounder. Saltwater fish was one of my favorite dishes, and Grandma always cooked it when she wanted to make me feel better.

I wondered who could be calling.

I picked up the phone. "Talk," I said.

"Is that the way you answer the phone?" the voice said.

"Identify yourself." I knew this wasn't a voice I was used to hearing.

"It's me—Brandy," she said.

"Oh." I was a little surprised to be hearing her voice so soon. Of course Mr. Tillman would pair me up with Brandy. Just my luck.

Brandy was breathing a little heavily into the phone, probably because of her weight, I guess. "I was calling to see if you found the answer to number six in the homework. I just can't figure that one out."

I let out a deep sigh. "Well, I haven't exactly looked at the homework yet," I told her. "Today's Tuesday, and it's not due till Friday."

Brandy laughed. "I guess you might say I am sort of an early bird."

"I'll say."

"I just don't like to wait too long to do my homework, or I'll forget what I've learned," she said in a nervous voice.

I was growing impatient and wanted to get off the phone. "Well, like I said, I haven't gotten to it yet," I said sternly.

Brandy interrupted. "How about we do our homework together?" she said excitedly. "We are homework buddies, remember?"

"My grandma is cooking dinner right now," I said.

"Great!" she responded. "I don't mind coming for dinner first, and then we can do our homework afterward."

"Brandy, wait!"

"Too late!" she said. "I'll see you at six!"

Brandy hung up the phone in a hurry. I guessed I had better tell Grandma Bean to set another place at the table. Darn, I thought, snapping my fingers; I wanted to have leftovers for tomorrow! Brandy showed up for dinner at 5:45 p.m. I must admit, I was kind of nervous with her being there and all. I mean, she did invite herself.

Brandy arrived dressed in black leather pants, an off-the-shoulder shirt, and a choker around her neck. She often wore her hair in braids pulled up in a ponytail. She had her books propped up on her hip as if the books were hanging on for dear life.

"Good Lord, girl," Brandy said. "It smells good in this house!" She walked in, literally moved me out of the way, and followed the smell. I just stood there in shock at how bold this girl was.

"Uh, yeah, you can come in," I said sarcastically.

Brandy had already made herself comfortable in the kitchen and was talking to Grandma Bean like she had known her all her life. Grandma was enjoying the conversation and tried to get me to join in too.

"Micah, you didn't tell me Brandy was an honor student," she said. "I'm so glad you're making some positive friends."

"Grandma, I have good friends already!"

Grandma Bean smacked her lips as she was turning over the fish. "A nosy girl and a dumb boyfriend do not count as friends," she responded.

I couldn't believe that my grandma was trying to embarrass me!

Grandma Bean wiped her mouth. "You and Brandy hurry up and wash your hands for dinner."

I motioned for Brandy to follow me upstairs to the bathroom. As I was washing my hands, I accidentally spilled water on Brandy's leather pants. She acted as if she wanted to say something to me.

I waited for her to react. "Got something you wanna say, girlie?" I asked. I knew Brandy was big enough to whup my tail, but I tested her anyway.

"No, Micah," she replied. "I guess you had an accident."

Then she swooped up a handful of water and splashed it on my chest. I could not believe she'd wet up my entire shirt. I was soaking wet! I marched downstairs and sat down at the dinner table. Brandy was right behind me and took her seat facing me. Grandma Bean turned around to see two wet kids sitting at her table. All I know is, I didn't crack a smile. I stared into Brandy's sneaky little eyes. She leaned back in her chair as if she owned the joint. Then she let out a slight smile at me. "Please pass the peas, Micah, because I sure am hungry," she said.

I knew this was going to be a long dinner. I took the bowl of peas and slammed it on the table. Just then Grandma Bean turned around and let me have it for slamming her green Tupperware bowl. Whap! Right across the head!

"Ouch!" I shouted.

Brandy began chuckling under her breath. Then she took her hand and tried to control her laughter by covering her mouth. I gave her a mean look, like she'd better stop laughing at me, or else. Then I heard the front door open and footsteps coming toward the kitchen.

"Anybody home?" a voice called out.

In came Pastor Jacobs with a big cheesy smile. Now if you wanna see a pit bull turn into a pussycat . . . whenever Pastor Jacobs dropped by, Grandma would melt away. Pastor Jacobs was the son Grandma had never had. Mama said Grandma Bean lost a baby boy at eight months. Mama said my granddad may have had something to do with it. Pastor Jacobs was Grandma Bean's best friend's son. Ms. Ida had been with the Lord since I was two.

In fact, Ms. Ida was the one who gave Grandma Bean her name. Word around town is, back in the day Grandma Bean and Ms. Ida used to run a bootleg hole just past James River. Ms. Ida was flashy and shaped liked a perfect Coca-Cola bottle. She could pull any man she wanted, and she did just that! Grandma was skinny, but still she was pretty. In black America, if you didn't have a big butt, you at least had big breasts, or you wasn't pulling nothing! Not no black man, anyhow! Poor, poor Grandma Bean. She was cursed; he didn't have either! Everybody said she looked like a beanpole, and thus came the name Bean. Some people called her C.B.—short for Camilla Bean—but all the young people called her Grandma Bean.

"Hello! Anybody home?" he called again.

"We in the kitchen, Tony," Grandma shouted back.

"Hey, there, what's going on C.B.? This food sure do look good," he said.

"Now, you know there is always an extra helping for you, sugar. Sit down and join us; we got plenty of food. I bet you ain't ate all day."

"I sure ain't, C.B."

"How come you always going to see about other folks, but you don't even take care of yourself?" Grandma asked. "You need a good Christian woman by your side that's gonna take good care of ya. That Lawrence girl ain't married yet. You reckon you might be interested in her?"

"Now, C.B., you know I am much too busy with starting up the different programs of the church right now. You know the community needs me."

Grandma Bean began fixing Pastor Jacobs a plate of food. "That don't mean you gotta be out there in the middle of the night passing out them there blankets and talking to them rotten drug dealers. You could get shot or even killed!"

"If I don't go out there, who will? These are the same stomping grounds I used to sell drugs on. I know this community better than anyone else. God sent me here for a reason."

Grandma Bean always managed to try to persuade Pastor Jacobs to stop going out in the middle of the night amongst the drug dealers and prostitutes. What Grandma Bean failed to realize was that Pastor Jacobs was not just an ordinary preacher; he actually practiced what he preached. Twenty years earlier, Pastor Jacobs used to be the number-one drug dealer in this tired old community. He was a big-timer, riding around in limousines and stuff, having people on his payroll from all over. Some of the men Pastor used to sell drugs with were still out there selling today—people like Woody who would never in a million years give up the game.

Word was that Woody set Pastor up when they were selling drugs together. Pastor was buying drugs from out of the country. He even had his own place where he had people making the drugs in Cuba. Pastor Jacobs and Woody were trying to make a deal with some people in New York. Come to find out the people they were dealing with were undercover officers and arrested both of them. Word was, they had been following Pastor Jacobs for years, waiting, trying to get something on him. Woody made a deal with the police and turned against Pastor Jacobs. Pastor Jacobs went to jail, and that was when his life began to change. To make a long story short, Pastor Jacobs found Jesus, and Woody continued working for the devil!

Pastor Jacobs was tearing up that fish! I was starting to get a little bit jealous because Brandy and Pastor Jacobs were on their third piece of fish, and I was still on my first.

Pastor Jacobs looked at Brandy. "Hey there, young lady. I've never seen you. Are you one of Micah's friends?"

I interrupted and replied, "She's just in my class, Pastor. Uh, we just have to do some homework together, that's all."

Then Brandy interrupted and said, "But we are starting to become friends. We've been spending a lot of time together." She turned to me and flashed a big cheesy smile. I could tell she was just eating all this up!

Grandma Bean intervened and started a conversation with Pastor. I just sat there, knowing that this girl had lost her everlasting mind. She think she slick old shyster! By the end of the dinner, Brandy had managed to get herself invited to church on Sunday by Pastor, and she took a plate of fish home for later.

The next few days in school, Brandy would sit beside me in class, trying to be nice, starting conversations and whatnot. I tried to be nice to her because Grandma said, "God sends people in your life for a reason." I wished I knew the reason for her being in my life. Brandy even tried to walk home with me. Forget a puppy; I had Brandy as my new pet, and she was definitely a pit bull! To my surprise, Brandy and Shana got along just perfect. Sometimes I told them both I'd like to walk home alone so that I could stop by me and Cherish's special place. They seemed to always understand. After all, dead or alive, Cherish was still my best friend, and nobody was going to take her place!

Chapter Six

"Micah, telephone!" Grandma Bean yelled.

"Grandma Bean, take a message," I shouted back. "I'm watching TV."

"Micah, it's your mother" she said in a stern voice. "Come downstairs right now!"

"Okay," I said. I really didn't want to talk to Mama. Besides the fact that she was in prison, she never fully admitted to taking the fall for Woody. I stormed downstairs in the worst manner possible. Grandma Bean put her hand on her hip with a look on her face that said, *Come get this phone!* I was hesitant to talk to Mama. I slowly picked up the phone and held it to my ear.

"Hello," I said.

"Hey, baby, how are you doing?" she said.

I sighed. "Fine."

"Well, you know I've been doing fine too!" she said. "I've been doing a lot of thinking about things, and I want you to know I've been hearing about you making new friends and all. I'm glad to see you are starting to get back into the swing of things. No use crying over spilled milk!"

"Excuse me?" I could not believe my ears. Was Mama referring to Cherish as spilled milk? I was stunned.

Mama cleared her voice. "What I mean to say is, we can't stay in the same healing spot forever. Micah, I want my family back, ya know?"

I felt myself becoming overwhelmed with anger. "What family, Mama?"

"Well, you know, Micah, it has always been me, you, and your Grandma Bean . . ."

Before Mama could continue on, I interrupted her. "Really, it has always been me and Grandma Bean."

Mama became upset and angry with me. "Oh, you want to go and blame everything on me, huh? I gave birth to you, girl! I'm the one who *chose* to have you. I didn't have to have you! I'm sitting in jail trying to make the best of things while you dogging me out. Is that the way your Lord say to treat your mama? No, I think your Bible say something about honoring thy mother and thy father. Since your father is long gone, you need to double your honor for me! As a matter of fact, every time you talk to me, you should begin with a "Yes, your honor." I mean, I am trying to have a better life. I am getting my GED up in here."

I held the phone in the air while she continued to talk. I was trying to keep my cool.

"Micah, you better answer me, girl," she said.

"Yes, Mommy Dearest?" I replied.

Mama paused for a second; I knew she hated that movie. "All I'm saying is that you need to hold on. I will be out of jail in a little bit. They can't keep me forever."

Was she for real? Jail is real. "Mama, maybe you need to take a look at some of those law books while you are in there. The judge sentenced you to life without the possibility of parole!"

"See, Micah, you don't know anything! Woody has a plan to get me out of here."

"Mama, *you ain't never getting out!*" I shouted. "Besides, nobody has even seen Woody since that night when everything happened."

Mama smacked her lips as if I was telling a lie. "Well, that's because it was just part of the plan."

I heard the phone pick up. "Yeah, God's plan," the voice said.

"Grandma Bean, is that you?" I asked.

"Well, I was just making sure that the phones were working right," Grandma Bean replied.

Mama let out a sigh on the phone. "Micah, will you ever forgive me?" she asked.

I took the phone away from my ear and gasped a deep breath. Truth is, I was nowhere near ready to forgive Mama. I slowly put the phone back to my ear. I felt like she'd chosen Woody over me. I was still just as angry with her as I was the day I found out she took the blame for murdering Cherish. How could I forgive her? How could I have a mother-daughter relationship with someone like that? "I . . . I don't think I can forgive you right now, Mama," I replied.

I hung up the phone before Mama could answer back. A sharp pain shot through my heart. Tears began streaming down my face. I heard footsteps behind me. It was Grandma Bean.

"Micah, it's okay to cry" she said. "Come over here, baby." I ran into her arms and held her tight, and she comforted me. I thanked God for Grandma Bean. What would I do without her?

Chapter Seven

The sky was blue and the trees were thirsty for water. I couldn't believe it was ninety-three degrees and Grandma Bean wanted me to shuck this corn on the hottest, most humid day in North Carolina. Sweat was racing down my face. I was seventeen years old now, too old to be doing this. I had grown into a shapely girl, as my grandma would say.

Grandma Bean came out on the porch, dressed in her shopping attire, topped with a sun hat and shades. "Micah, you finish that corn up. I'm going to the wig store. Matter of fact, take Rochelle about two freezer bags full of corn. Those children of hers could use some proper nutrition."

"Yes, ma'am," I replied.

Now, I don't know why Grandma Bean continues to send food over there all the time. Ms. Rochelle's usually too "high" to eat it. I bet Ms. Rochelle got the thickest file in social services. They've only been nice to her because her mama retired from that office. They could have been done and took them kids from her. Ms. Rochelle had a lot of kids too, five to be exact, and one on the way. Sometimes Shana and Brandy would come to my house, and we'd just watch the show next door. We sat on the porch and watched Ms. Rochelle cuss out the social worker. It was cheaper and better than going to the movies.

As soon as I finished shucking and cleaning the corn, I placed them in freezer bags. My hands were filthy, and I couldn't keep any nails for shucking all the time. I headed over to Ms. Rochelle's house. Her whole yard looked nasty and creepy. The house looked liked a shack out of a third world country. Even the dog didn't bark right. You could see the skin and bones off that dog, and I knew she wasn't feeding Shelby. I tossed the dog a couple of ears of corn. She ate that corn fast and fierce too. Poor Shelby, she looked so weak and had a bit of a limp. I don't know why she got that dog if she wasn't gonna take care of it. I got a good mind to call the animal control people on her. Drug addicts are not supposed to have a dog. I hesitated to knock on the door. I swear I didn't feel like hearing Rochelle's mouth.

"Rochelle!" I yelled through the screen door, hoping she would meet me at the door.

"Rochelle, you in there? It's Micah from across the street!" I didn't hear anything. I hoped she ain't gone and died up in this house. I put down the corn and tiptoed around to the back of the house. Maybe I could see into Rochelle's bedroom window if I stood on the garbage can. Shelby followed me around, twitching her head from side to side, trying to figure out what I was doing. Poor doggy. I just might take her from Rochelle.

There I was, standing on top of a garbage can, looking into a crackhead's house. I tipped my head up just enough to see into her bedroom window.

"Boo!" a voice said through the window.

I screamed as loud as I could before falling off the trash can and hitting the ground hard. I think I broke my tailbone. I heard a woman's laughter and looked up. It was Rochelle staring down at me. Now I was pissed. "Girl, why you scare me like that?"

Rochelle looked at me like I was crazy. "Why you all up in my house?" she asked.

"I just wanna give ya some corn. Can a sista give you some corn?"

Rochelle burst out laughing. Her hair was wild, and her clothes were dingy. She looked as if she had been up for days. "You wanna give me some corn through my bedroom window?" she asked. She smacked her lips as if she didn't believe me. "You ain't no Peeping Tom, are you, Micah? I see the way you look at me. I only turn tricks for men, not women!"

Oh, no, she didn't! "Girl, I ain't gay!" I replied. "Trust me, you ain't got nothing I want to see."

Rochelle let out a big laugh. "Girl, I'm just kidding with you. Come around the front. I'll let you in. And be quiet; my kids are sleeping."

I went around to the front porch. I picked up the bags of corn and waited for Rochelle to open the screen door.

"Aw, looka there, Micah brung me some corn. What I look like, a pig?" she asked.

Aside from Rochelle's horrible attitude, she had to be the most ungrateful bitty I had ever met. "Yes, yes, you do, as a matter of fact," I replied.

Rochelle hit me on the arm. I dropped the corn down on the table. Rochelle looked over the corn as if she was inspecting it. "Did Grandma Bean send this for me? She always looking out for me. Could you tell her next time send me some meat? My food stamps ain't come in yet, and I need to feed these kids."

She was asking a lot for someone who never gave us nothing. "They ain't got no daddy?" I asked.

Rochelle grew angry about that. "Watch your mouth, girl. I'm thirty-one years old. You need to respect me."

"I ain't mean nothing by it," I said. "Just asking, that's all."

"Yeah, well, I'm they mama and they daddy," she said. "It's hard doing this by yourself. These kids keep on stressing me every day. Sometimes I just need something to calm me down."

Rochelle walked toward the living room and stared at an old picture of her mama. "When Mama was alive, she took care of all of us. We ain't never wanted for nothing."

I walked over to the picture and picked it up. "Sulla was a mighty fine lady," I said.

Rochelle gave me a mean look and snatched the picture from my hands. "It's *Mrs. Sulla May* to you. My mama was the best worker at social services. She was on the school board, church choir, and all sorts of committees. Yes, my mama did it all. Everybody loved my mama. Nobody didn't mess with her! Why, if she was alive today, she would cuss them crackers out down there at social services. Who do they think they are, trying to take my babies? I'll shoot them up 'fore that happens! My mama wouldn't dare let them mess with me."

I felt bad for Rochelle. She didn't have anyone since her mom died. No man wanted nothing to do with her, because she smoked dope and was loose. "You know," I said, "I bet if Ms. Sulla was alive, she would help you, Rochelle."

Rochelle paused for a second, then put the picture back down on the table. Rochelle gave me a crazy look like I had crossed the line or something. "Your mama help you?" she said in a mean voice.

I paused. No, she didn't even go there! That was it for me. "Bye, Rochelle!"

I stormed out of the home, slamming the door behind me. That was why I didn't like going over there!

It was late when Grandma Bean came back home. I heard some footsteps creeping in the kitchen. That was not like Grandma Bean. I really don't like being in the house alone. It's been years, but I still have nightmares sometimes about what happened to Cherish. I tiptoed downstairs, but I still didn't see Grandma Bean anywhere. "Grandma Bean, is that you?" I asked.

"Yeah, it's me, baby," she said. "I just got in a little late." She didn't look her normal self. She looked tired and worn out. I kneeled down to help her take her shoes off. "Grandma Bean, are you okay?" I asked.

Grandma responded in a tired voice. "Yeah, Micah."

"Micah, baby, there is something I want to talk to you about," she said.

"What's going on, Grandma?" I knew by the look on her face that it was important. I was almost afraid to know what she had to talk to me about.

"Well, Micah, I have been feeling a little sick and . . ."

Just then, the phone rang. Grandma Bean went to pick it up. I don't know which was better, knowing what she had to tell me, or not knowing.

"Yeah, I'll accept charges," she said into the phone.

I knew it was Mama when Grandma Bean said she would accept charges. Of course, I was nosey and listened at the telephone conversation. Grandma Bean tried to lower her voice to keep me from listening.

"No, I haven't told her yet, but I will be by on Sunday. We'll see you on Sunday, Rose."

I hoped Grandma Bean didn't include me in the "we" category. I just wasn't ready to face Mama yet. I still hadn't forgiven her for what she did. I heard Grandma hang up the phone, and she came back over to the couch were I was. I pretended to flip the TV channels as if I was looking for something to watch.

"You busy watching television, girl? I need to finish talking with you." I turned off the TV and directed my attention toward her. "Micah, I think it's time you go visit your mama. You almost a grown woman now."

Grandma Bean was right. Time had flown by. I was growing up faster than a weed. But I still didn't think I was ready to see Mama.

"What, Grandma Bean? How come you want me to go and visit a murderer?" I asked.

She paused for a second. "Your mama didn't murder anybody, and you know that, girl."

"Hm . . . she might as well have murdered Cherish, because she took the blame for it."

"Micah, God has called us to forgive one another. He didn't say forgive some and not the others; he said to forgive anybody." She took off her wig and began brushing at it.

"Well, he didn't mean Mama," I said. "Nobody can forgive her for what she done—oh fat liar!"

Grandma Bean slammed her wig down on the chair. "Micah, she is still your mother and my daughter!" she shouted. "I don't want to hear you talk like that in my house. You know what—the devil is steady working in you. You all fired up and angry at the world, still all these years later. Until you let God come into your life and forgive your mama, you ain't gonna have no peace!" She began crying. It was almost like she was sobbing. She just lifted her hands up to the air as if she was saying, *Lord help me!*

I went over to Grandma Bean and hugged her. I couldn't say anything. A tear rolled down my cheek and hit the floor. I felt like that tear that dropped. I felt like I was falling. I want to be happy and free, but the anger I had for Mama almost consumed me.
Grandma Bean rubbed my back to comfort me. "Micah, you about to be a grown woman soon. I just pray that whatever happens to me, the Spirit of the Lord will always be with you. Honey, I just want you to know you'll never be alone."

I lifted my head and faced her. "I know God is with me, Grandma Bean," I said.

"Yeah, baby, but one day you will know him for yourself." Then she picked her wig up from the chair, placed it on her head, and went outside on the porch. I could hear her singing church hymns. She would always sing a song when she didn't know what to do. I know she wanted me to forgive Mama, but that was going to be a process.

I was sitting in the hair salon, getting my hair done for church the next day. No matter how hard things were, Grandma Bean always made sure my hair was done for church. My hair was long and thick by then, and I must admit, it was one of my prized possessions. I was never able to cut my hair, because Grandma Bean didn't believe women should wear short haircuts.

Sometimes I would experiment with my own hair; I did have skills. I began doing hair on the side. Most of the high school kids knew who to come to in order to get their hair done for cheaper prices than the beauty salon. Brandy was always at my house getting her hair done in different styles. Shana would get an edge up, because she sports a sleek natural.

Times had changed. Shana was into "black pride." She was even visiting historically black universities to pursue her bachelor's degree. Shana claimed she wasn't sure what to major in, but whatever it would be, she'd use her degree to bring up the African American community. I must say, she had grown into a rather ambitious young lady.

She still had a big mouth, though. Yesterday she told Linwood I was still a virgin. I don't think it bothered Linwood, though. I think I was proud of the fact I was still a virgin. I couldn't believe all the time we had known each other, we never actually went all the way. Anyway, I collected my thoughts as I saw Grandma Bean's car pulling up.

Grandma Bean tapped the head of the hairdryer to get my attention. "Micah, you through yet?" she asked.

"No, ma'am. I have about fifteen more minutes."

Grandma Bean looked at her watch, "Well, I'll be back to get you. I'm going to pay some more bills."

"Okay," I replied.

While I was getting my hair styled, I overheard some of the other beauticians talking about Rochelle. I heard one of them say Rochelle wasn't nothing but a junkie.

Carmen, my beautician, jumped into the conversation. Carmen was a red-boned girl, quite independent, owning her shop—being a woman and all. "Now, y'all know y'all should not be talking about that girl. Drugs are a hard thing to kick."

She told them to drop the conversation, but Lena, another beautician, carried on with the conversation.

Carmen stood there with her hand on her hips. "Lena, just drop the subject!"

I could tell Carmen was getting upset about the continued gossiping. Carmen didn't allow that in her beauty shop. Carmen was a Christian woman, trying to run a Christian business.

Lena smacked her lips because she could not believe Carmen had cut her off. She loved to gossip and was having a hard time doing so in Carmen's shop. She was a skinny girl—too skinny to be Latina, they say. "Look, Carmen, I'm just saying, it's one thing if she does drugs, but how she gonna work for Woody?"

Something inside me jumped. I couldn't believe my ears! Carmen stopped brushing my hair. Carmen knew that was one name I didn't want to hear. I did not like to hear anything about Woody; his name alone would haunt me. I'd thought I would never hear that name again. I had finally started trying to put the past in the past, and now he was back?

"Did you say *Woody?*" I asked Lena.

Lena looked at the confused look on my face. She didn't know whether to confirm or deny the fact that Rochelle was working for Woody. She looked nervous. "I . . . I heard Rochelle was turning tricks for Woody," she replied. "My boyfriend said Woody is back in town, just keeping things on the down-low."

I sat back in the chair and started talking to myself. *Relax, relate, release, Micah.* I repeated this chant. I tried to remember what the therapist taught me after Cherish died. The mere mention of Woody's name turned my stomach. I was disgusted on the inside. I had not seen or heard from Woody since Cherish died and he disappeared. I couldn't believe he had the nerve to come back to town.

"Finish my hair, Carmen!" I said.

By the time Carmen had actually finished my hair, I was more heated than ever. I stormed out of the beauty shop. I was so angry, I began running home. All I could think about was how Grandma Bean always had me taking that hussy a portion of our food—and she was working for Woody? That hussy knew what Woody was doing to our family, and she had the nerve to be working for him! Rochelle was playing me and Grandma Bean.

I cut through several yards so I could get to Rochelle's house quicker. Linwood was outside on his porch with his friends. I paid him no mind. My focus was on kicking Rochelle's butt. Linwood knew I was mad, and so did his boys. They had witnessed plenty of arguments between me and Linwood.

"Micah, what is wrong with you?" Linwood asked.

I looked behind me to find Linwood and his boys following me.

"Not now, Linwood!" I shouted. "I'm about to open up a can of whup-ass on Rochelle. That hussy done messed with the wrong girl!"

I heard the boys in the background yelling, "Fight, fight!"

Before I knew it, a whole crowd had joined in, following me to Rochelle's house. Everybody wanted to see what was going to happen. Rochelle might be bigger than me, but I was so mad, I could definitely hurt her. My first thought was to take a bottle and bust it upside her head. I have a motto: don't fight fair. By the time I got to Rochelle's house, I didn't even notice all the cars there. I just began looking on the ground for a bottle. I wasn't going to fight fair, but I was going to fight!

Linwood and his boys kept shouting my name, but I was focused on looking for a weapon. I just ignored them and broke me off a piece of glass bottle for battle. Then I saw Brandy and Shana too. They ran toward me. Suddenly I noticed all the people at Rochelle's house. There were state cars, policemen, and an ambulance. All the neighbors were crowded around. Rochelle was hollering and screaming at them.

Rochelle was filthy dirty. Her shorts were dingy, and her shirt that had once been white was soiled with stains. She looked like she had been on a drug binge. She was quite fidgety and was screaming and yelling. "Don't take my children!" she kept shouting.

Rochelle looked like she was out of control. She was barely focusing and was slurring her words. The social worker had the children in her car, and the policemen were trying to restrain Rochelle from getting to them.

I finally stopped and asked Brandy, "What's going on?"

Brandy looked at me with tears in her eyes. "They taking Rochelle's kids. The social worker came by the house and caught Rochelle using cocaine. The kids were home at the time. I guess this was the final straw." She was sobbing.

Shana started crying and appeared sad. I actually felt sorry for Rochelle. At that moment, I realized she was her own worst enemy. I didn't doubt Rochelle loved her children, but the drug was more powerful than her will. Drugs had become her god. Linwood finally caught up to me. He could see I was in shock.

"I can't believe they taking her kids away!" he said.

"Me either, Linwood."

I felt bad because just moments earlier I wanted to fight her. I wanted to rip her face off! I could hear Rochelle pleading with everyone to not take her kids. Rochelle cried and at times became violent with law enforcement. It was a cry I'd never heard from a woman before. It was a cry from a mother. A deep wailing cry, where her soul hurt. See, when a woman cries, her heart hurts; but when a mother cries, her soul hurts. I dropped my head in shame. I felt so bad for her. Forgive me, Lord. That's all I can say.

Chapter Eight

I was still completely in shock as to everything that had happened earlier that day with Rochelle. Nothing like that had ever happened in our community. I lay on the couch just to try to relax. How could so much happen in one day? I took a deep breath and fell asleep.

I fell into a deep dream and saw Cherish sitting under our favorite tree. She was dressed all in white. There was land. A river divided the land into two. I called out her name, but she didn't respond. I started running toward her, but I was stopped by the river. Cherish was on the other side of the river. It was like I couldn't reach her. She looked at me and then held out her arms, but I couldn't reach her; I couldn't get close to her.

Cherish looked as if she felt sorry for me. Her arms were opened, but she was sad because she wasn't able to embrace me. Her hands slowly opened and there in the palm of her hand was a tiny cross made of gold. She threw the cross over to me as if she was throwing a life jacket for my rescue. Funny thing is, as the cross came over to my side, it became larger and larger in size. I was afraid to pick up the cross, so I just let it lay there on the green grass. I didn't touch it or move it. Suddenly, I heard my name being called.

"Micah, Micah!" the voice said.

My eyelids began to open, and I realized it was just a dream. I stumbled to the front door to see who it was. It was Brandy and Shana.

"Girl, why you sweating so hard?" Shana asked. There was a disgusted look on her face.

"It was hot and I fell asleep on the couch. I guess I must have sweated a little in my sleep. Y'all come in."

"We were worried about you. Carmen called me to see if I had seen you. She told me what happened at the salon. We know about Woody and Rochelle. Are you okay?" Shana asked.

Brandy grabbed my hand and squeezed it. I could tell she was really worried about my feelings. "Are you?" she asked.

"Yeah, I guess I was just in shock to find out Woody was back in town," I replied. "I never expected to hear about him again."

Shana twirled around in the recliner chair, popping the gum in her mouth. Sometimes I felt as though she was just a big kid! I loved her, though. I loved both them girls like sisters. I had not let anyone get as close to me since Cherish died.

I guess God knew I needed someone in my life. Just then, I heard the screeching of brakes in the driveway. Grandma Bean busted in the door, looking worried.

"Micah, I have been looking all over for you! Why didn't you wait at the beauty shop for me to pick you up?" she asked.

"Carmen didn't tell you what happened?" I asked.

"Yeah . . . and . . . ?"

I figured Grandma Bean had not heard about Rochelle working for Woody. She couldn't have, to be acting this calm. She must have thought me and Rochelle just had a disagreement or something.

"Rochelle been working for Woody and—"

Grandma Bean interrupted. "And that don't have nothing to do with you. That ain't no reason for you to fight that girl! That girl is caught up in drugs, which resulted in her working for Woody!"

"You mean you ain't mad?" I asked.

"I gave that food for her and them babies," Grandma said. "I don't take that back. If folks want to do wrong and think they getting something over on people, then they have to answer to God for that. Everything always comes out in the end. I wouldn't waste my time trying to fight her or Woody. God can do more than my fist will ever do. You can't mess over a child of God and expect to get away with it! Now, you girls fix you a snack, and for God-sakes put the air condition on! I'll be back in a jiffy. I have a couple of errands to run."

Grandma Bean picked up her purse, kissed me on the forehead, and dashed out the door. Brandy, Shana, and I were all speechless. Grandma Bean never ceased to amaze me.

I collapsed and fell down on the chair next to Brandy and Shana. Grandma Bean was a very forgiving woman. Sweat dripped down from my forehead to my knees. I looked over at Shana and Brandy. They seemed to be sweating hard also.

"Y'all hot?" I asked.

Brandy gave me a look. "What do you think? Of course, we hot. It feels like its a hundred degrees in here."

"Well, why y'all didn't say so?" I said.

Brandy started fanning herself and said, "I guess we figured you would get the hint, seeing all our clothes dripping wet like this. Y'all skinny girls might love the heat, but a big girl like me needs some cool air."

Shana cut her eyes at Brandy. Shana was self-conscious about her slim weight. She wore a size two, and if she wore boxers under her jeans, she could get into a size three or four. Shana had the body of a white girl. The only problem was, she was black. A black girl with no breast or butt don't get much play around here. Brandy was a big girl. I mean, she's not obese or anything, but she's just big. Brandy is tall with big breast, big thighs, long legs, and a small waste. She's like Foxy Brown or something. I have to admit, even I am intimidated walking beside her in the mall.

Shana headed for the kitchen and threw a pillow at Brandy. "Brandy, for your info, some of us are gaining weight," she said.

Brandy gave Shana the hand and giggled under her breath. She knew she'd struck a nerve with Shana. "You still skinnier than a toothpick," she said.

Of course, you know I had to throw my two cents in. After all, I may not have any breast, but I do have a big butt. I got up and started dancing, shaking my butt in the air. Round and round my butt went in circles.

Shana and Brandy joined in on the living room floor, shaking their rumps. Round and round they went. I was careful not to bump Brandy, because I was afraid she might knock me down. Brandy swayed her hips while singing that she had a big butt. She bumped Shana clear across the living room floor. Shana landed flat on her bottom. We all fell out, laughing hysterically on the living room floor. We couldn't even catch our breath. A serious look came upon Brandy's face. She opened her arms and pulled me and Shana inward, flinging us against her breasts.

"You guys promise me we will stay friends no matter what," she said.

I could barely see Shana's face over Brandy's boobs. "We promise," I said.

Shana and I could barely breathe, because Brandy's breast was cutting off our air supply.

"Brandy," I said.

"Yeah, Micah?"

"We love you, but right now we can't breathe."

Brandy looked downward and realized she was smothering us. She relaxed her arms and Shana fell to the ground gasping for air. Then we both looked at each other and burst out laughing all over again.

Chapter Nine

Church was off-the-hook this morning! The choir was singing and the drums were so loud you could feel it in yourself. People were shouting and running up and down the aisle. Even Shana and Brandy were standing up, clapping their hands and rocking to the beat. Brandy's hands kept bumping into Shana's hands. Shana would stop and give her an evil look. Brandy would just try to move over some. It was tight up in there! I was afraid the church was going to pop! Pastor Jacobs did the altar call next. He would always start off by saying, "Is today your day?" I looked out of the corner of my eye to see Linwood creeping out the church door.

Pastor Jacobs asked if anyone needed prayer. I felt like going up there for prayer. I felt as if a hand was pushing up against my back. Pastor Jacobs started talking about how the Lord forgives us for what we have done.

"Some of y'all need healing from your past," he said. "You carrying around baggage that's weighing you down. How can you move closer to God if you can't forgive yourselves? Come to Jesus right now, so he can give you rest."

Pastor Jacobs's words were powerful. All around, I could hear the footsteps walking down the aisle. I knew I should be one of them. That pressure was on my back again. Only I couldn't take my hands off the pew. I couldn't move at all. Suddenly I felt someone poking me in my side.

It was Brandy poking at me. "Psst, you going down there?" she said.

Brandy looked at me as if she wanted me to say yes. Only I couldn't say yes. Not even God could forgive me for what I done to Cherish. If it wasn't for me, she would be living. I was ashamed to stand in the sight of God. I was better off in the darkness.

"Naw, girl, God ain't ready for me yet," I replied. "Besides, I ain't perfect like Grandma Bean."

"You right, girl. I ain't ready neither," she said. "I was just checking to see what you was gonna do."

I closed my eyes again, then opened one eye to see who was coming down the aisle to the altar. It was a woman in fishnet stockings and a one-piece miniskirt. The smell of alcohol strolled closely behind her. I lifted up my head so I could see her face. It was Rochelle. Her eyes were bloodshot red, and she sort of swayed while trying to stand. Then she leaned toward Pastor Jacobs and whispered the words, "I need prayer."

Pastor Jacobs patted her on the shoulders as if he agreed.

Suddenly I felt a slap on the head. I looked up to see it was Grandma Bean. "Micah, close them eyes 'fore I pop you again," she said.

I guess next time I need to be more careful when I am peeking. Grandma Bean waited for my response. "Do you hear me, young lady?" she asked.

"Yes, ma'am, I hear you loud and clear," I replied.

I could hear Brandy snickering. Then she choked on her own spit. That's what she got for laughing at me!

On the way home from church, Grandma Bean was unusually quiet. Normally, she would have talked to everyone and their mama after church. I was surprised when she went straight to the car. I could tell she was thinking about something. She even had on her best Sunday dress and kept on mumbling gospel hymns under her breath. I just zoned out into my own world. Soon I noticed we were passing the exit to our house.

"Where are we going?" I asked.

Grandma Bean stayed silent and kept driving. After a while, I noticed we were coming up on the state prison exit. Grandma focused on driving, trying to ignore me, but she knew I was confused.

"Micah, we going to see your mama," she said. "Is some things we all need to discuss. Pastor Jacobs is going to meet us there, just to be a support."

I didn't know if I was ready to see Mama. I didn't know if Mama was ready to see me. Grandma Bean patted me on the hand. "Micah, I'm going to be right there with you," she assured me.

I knew one day I would have to face Mama, but I hadn't known it would be *that* day. I don't know what to say to Mama. I was not prepared for this. As we drove up, I looked around the prison to see guards everywhere. It looked so sad. How could Mama's life have ended up like this?

Pastor Jacobs was outside waiting on us. Grandma Bean parked the car and began taking off her seatbelt. She looked over at me and gave me a faint smile.

"Everything is going to be all right," she said.

Grandma Bean got out of the car to greet Pastor Jacobs. I didn't know if I was ready for this, but I was about to find out. Pastor Jacobs walked me into the room where Mama was. She looked as if she'd lost weight. Her hair was shorter, and she seemed to be calm. Grandma Bean sat down beside me.

Pastor Jacobs held my hand the whole time. Mama looked at me and smiled. "Micah, your are getting so big," she said.

I said nothing. I laid my head on Pastor Jacobs, turning away from Mama. Pastor Jacobs patted me on the hand. I could tell Mama was disappointed because I didn't respond to her.

Grandma Bean interrupted and started talking to Mama. "How you been, Rose?" she asked.

Mama looked at me in disappointment before answering Grandma Bean. "I've been doing just fine, Mama. I got my life together, and I'm doing well. I even got my GED, thanks to Allah."

Mama was talking to Grandma Bean yet looking at me. Grandma looked confused.

"Allah?" she asked.

Even though I wasn't doing well, I could tell Grandma Bean was upset when Mama said, "thanks to Allah." Grandma Bean has always said there's only one God you can serve.

"You better forget about Allah and look to Jesus with all the trouble you in, girl!" she said.

In my mind, I was sort of thinking *Allah* meant *God.*

Pastor Jacobs just shook his head. Now I knew Pastor Jacobs was going to say something, because he never held his tongue about anything.

"Now, Bean, I didn't know you had a fool for a daughter," he said.

Mama took offense to Pastor Jacob's comment. "I ain't no fool, Pastor! Everybody is entitled to the path they choose and the master they choose to serve. Anyway, Allah helped me to realize how much I love my daughter and how much she needs me to be in her life right now." She directed her attention toward me. "Baby, next month you'll be eighteen. I know I wasn't there for a big part of your life. I hope that you can forgive me. I know this isn't the best situation, but like I said, I hope we can start from this day forth. Like I said, Allah has really guided my life in a new direction. What do ya say?"

I couldn't believe my mom was saying all this. Mama acted as if she could make everything okay just because she supposedly changed her life. I was so angry, smoke was coming out of my ears. Mama looked at me as if she was puzzled about what could make me so mad.

"Micah, I'm waiting for an answer," she said.

I took a deep breath. Pastor Jacobs and Grandma Bean were waiting to see what I was going to say. The tension was so thick, you could cut it with a knife.

"It took Allah for you to realize you should have been a mother to me?" I shouted. "Well, that's a damn shame!"

I got up and ran out of the room. I felt so many emotions—embarrassment, anger—and on top of that, I had just cussed in front of the Pastor!

Chapter Ten

It's been a few days since I visited Mama in jail. I don't ever want to go back there again. Grandma Bean said she wouldn't take me to see Mama again if I didn't want to. She said she didn't want none of Mama's evil spirits jumping off on me. I tried to busy my mind, preparing for graduation. I planned on enrolling in cosmetology school during the spring of next year. I continued doing hair on the side, and I must admit, people loved the way I did their hair.

I still let Carmen do my hair. After working on everyone else's head, I didn't have any energy to do my own. Shana and Brandy were on their way over so we could pick out our graduation outfits. Shana was having a party after graduation, and we needed to look good. Shana said the host should always look good. I laid out all my best outfits. Shana even went to the thrift stores for special scarves and jackets they don't make any more. It wasn't a surprise that she wanted to major in fashion and design.

I went downstairs to see if we had enough treats in the refrigerator. Hm . . . brownies, rice crispy treats, pickles, and some leftover deviled eggs. Yeah, there was enough to snack on for the time being. Grandma Bean was busy sweeping the kitchen floor. Usually that was my job, but Grandma Bean was so happy I was graduating from high school, she'd let my chores slide for the week.

"You know this is supposed to be your job," she said.

"Yeah, Grandma Bean," I replied. "I need all my energy to march across the stage on graduation day."

Grandma Bean chuckled. She always knew when I was trying to get out of something.

"You are really growing up, baby. You certainly are becoming quite a woman."

I could tell Grandma Bean was really proud. After all, she did raise me by herself. I never got to meet Grandpa. Grandpa died before I was born. I never met my father, either. My dad was killed before I was born too. Sometimes I believe Mama really didn't know who my daddy was and just told me that so I wouldn't try to find out who he was. I realized right then that it was going to be my mission in life to be nothing like Mama. I refused to be a town drunk, and my children were gonna know who their father was. I looked at Grandma Bean with a serious look on my face.

"Grandma Bean, I'm gonna be somebody!" I said proudly. "I'm gonna be a hair stylist, and one day I'll own a salon. I'm sure gonna make a whole lot of money, and you gonna have a new hairstyle every week."

Grandma Bean looked at me and smiled.

"Honey, you can be anything you want to be with God. Remember that. You're gonna make a fine hair stylist. Girl, you gonna have old Grandma Bean looking good. Then I won't have to wear these tired old wigs!"

Grandma Bean and I laughed. Deep in my heart, I generally meant what I said. Grandma Bean always paid to have my hair done and never got her own hair done. Sometimes I felt like she'd given me everything she couldn't give Mama. She always made sure I was happy and gave me too much of her time and attention. She and I were a team. I didn't know what I would have done without her.

I figured Brandy and Shana would arrive thirty minutes late, as usual. Shana was eager for me to set her hair in a twist set. She loved for everyone to think her hair was naturally curly. It was actually naturally nappy! Grandma Bean always says black people don't have nappy hair. Brandy brung a couple of outfits; she was indecisive about what to wear. We all wanted to be color-coordinated in purple and pink. Shana had a skirt and top. Brandy showed off a full-body dress. Brandy flipped and tugged on the outfits, then tossed them aside and flipped the bed. She looked puzzled, as if she was actually thinking about something.

"What's wrong, Brandy?" I asked.

She looked back at me, and dropped the smile from her face.

"Nothing, man," she said. "Ain't nothing wrong with me."

"You sure, girl? You know you could talk to us about anything," I said.

Brandy positioned herself on my bed, flinging her arms behind her back and crossing her legs. She looked up at the ceiling and then looked back down again.

"Everything . . . it's gonna change between us," she said.

I stopped styling Shana's hair and went over to sit down on the bed beside Brandy. I could tell Brandy was genuinely worried about our friendship ending. I patted Brandy on the arms as if to reassure her somehow our friendship wouldn't end.

"Honey, our friendship will never end," I said.

"Yes, it will. Shana's going off to some fancy black school, and you gonna be heading to that beauty school, and what do I have? Nothing! I won't be able to do nothing, nothing at all, because I messed up!"

I looked over at Shana licking on a Tootsie Roll Pop. She rarely paid Brandy any attention at all. After all, Brandy was the dramatic one.

"What do you mean, *messed up?*"

Brandy rolled off my bed and squatted Indian-style on the floor.

"I'm—I'm pregnant, y'all!" she shouted.

I stopped combing Shana's hair. Shana's Tootsie Roll Pop fell out of her mouth and onto the ground.

"Pregnant?" Shana said. The word came out of her mouth like it was a plague.

I couldn't believe Brandy was pregnant. "Are you sure?" I asked.

Brandy looked at me as if she was surprised the question came out of my mouth. "Of course, I'm sure!" she said. "Do you think I would just make up something like this? I can just feel the little one swimming inside of me, probably trying to find a place to sleep."

Brandy rubbed her stomach as if she was nine-months pregnant, talking to a full-grown fetus.

"How pregnant are you?" Shana asked.

Shana and I couldn't really tell if Brandy was one month or nine months, being as though she was kind of thick and all.

Brandy hopped to her feet excitedly, as if she had a major announcement to make.

"I'm two months," she said. "Two months full pregnant."

I was a bit confused and needed some clarity.

"Who's the baby's daddy?" I asked.

Brandy took a deep breath. This was not good.

"It's between Jackson and Robby," she said. "I'm sure of it!"

Jackson and Robby were two cousins that attended our high school. They shared cars, clothes, and sometimes women.

Brandy wasn't embarrassed by the fact she had no idea who her baby's father was. The look on Shana's face was one of total disgust. I really didn't know what to say except the truth: I was totally disappointed in Brandy. How could she let herself get knocked up? The whole time we had known each other, she'd never had a steady boyfriend. No man would claim her as their girlfriend. I just couldn't figure out why she didn't have any more respect for herself. Brandy looked pitiful, acted pitiful, and was pitiful.

For the next few moments, everyone just stared at each other, pondering how this baby, which was coming in seven months, would change our friendship circle forever. Mostly, I felt sorry for Brandy. She was already living in the housing projects with her aunt. Now a baby would add to an already impoverished family. I was tempted to suggest to Brandy that her parents help out with the baby, but I didn't ask her about her mom and dad. Brandy never talked about her parents. I just left the situation alone and decided I would be there for her if she needed me. I took a deep breath and grabbed Brandy's hand, squeezing it tightly. Shana sat beside Brandy also, grabbing and squeezing her other hand, trying to comfort her in her own way. I looked at Brandy and Shana. They were my two best friends and nothing was gonna tear us apart.

"No matter what, we will always be there for you," I said. Shana agreed and hugged Brandy, squeezing her tightly.

Tears began rolling down Brandy's cheek. "You guys are more than friends," she said. "You have become my sisters. I love you both so much."

At that point, Shana and I burst into tears, sobbing continuously. Shana and I looked at each other. It was a unanimous decision about how we felt at that moment. We looked at each other as if to see if our thoughts were the same before mumbling, "We love you too, Brandy!"

And just like that, on that very day, our friendship went to a whole new level.

Chapter Eleven

It had to be the hottest summer ever. It was simply amazing how July could be so much hotter than June. I sat on the porch, looking up at the sun as its rays continued to kiss my black skin. No matter what I did, I could not hide from those persistent rays. The weather was a dry ninety-seven degrees, and the heat dried my long hair until it was almost brittle. I decided I would take advantage of the summer and just relax. Grandma Bean didn't push me to work. I could tell she was proud of me for being accepted into beauty college.

Grandma Bean had money put away for my education. Thank God, she didn't get discouraged by my C-average grades. Even Mama, in all her efforts, sent cards and balloons congratulating my accomplishments in high school. At that point in my life, I felt like the world was mine, and no one could ever stop me. Grandma Bean always said you could do anything with Jesus. Linwood and I decided to break up for the summer. Although he was finally a senior, he was now twenty years old, and quite frankly, that was embarrassing. I must admit, he still looked good, though, with his *fine* self. Yep, it was my time to shine!

I could see Brandy walking up the street to my house. She was really showing now. That girl was always somewhere. It didn't matter how hot or cold it was. Her aunt never let her use her car for nothing. She treated her own kids way better that she treated Brandy.

"Hey, girl," I said.

Brandy waved at me. I waved back at her. Her new growth was literally holding onto her braids. Her braids seemed as though they were unraveling and appeared old-looking. She looked hot. The sun had turned her skin into black coffee. Funny . . . I thought she would have been way fatter than she was by then, but her belly was the only thing that grew. She finally made it to the porch and sat down. She wiped the sweat off her forehead.

"Whew, girl! Sure is hot out here," she said.

Brandy looked tired, and I was concerned about her and the baby in that heat. "Let's go inside where it's cool," I said. "I'll fix you something to drink."

"I could use something to quench my thirst," she replied readily.

I helped Brandy off the porch and into the house. She flopped down in the recliner, propping her legs up. I fixed her and me some lemonade. She quickly washed it down and motioned me to get more. She took another sip of the lemonade and set the glass down. I picked up one of her braids, examining it carefully. I couldn't stand to see a woman's hair not kept up. I was now doing my own hair and assisting Carmen at the beauty shop. Carmen allowed me to wash hair in exchange for pay. It was under-the-table, of course, and best of all, it didn't feel like work. Seeing Brandy's' hair like this hurt my eyes, let alone my heart. I couldn't stand looking at her hair no longer, and I was about to bust.

"Girl, when you gonna let me do something to that head?" I said.

Brandy giggled; she knew nappy hair bothered me. "Look, Micah, you're not supposed to get a perm while you're

97

pregnant. The chemicals could sink into your scalp and poison the baby. Don't you know anything?"

"Now, I ain't never heard of such a thing," I said. Carmen had gotten a relaxer when she was pregnant, and ain't nothing happened to her baby. Brandy looked at me with a serious look on her face, took a big gulp of her lemonade, and set the half-empty glass down. Then she leaned in close to me as if she was going to tell me a secret.

"Carmen, my dear, is an alien," she said.

Brandy and I burst out laughing hysterically.

"You crazy, girl," I said.

All of sudden, Brandy's jaw dropped. She looked as if she was surprised by something outside.

"Brandy, what is it?" I asked.

"Oh, my God, guess who's back from rehab," she said, pointing outside.

"Who?" I asked. I ran to the door to see who it was.

"Rochelle!" she said.

Chapter Twelve

The clouds grew dark, and it started to rain hard outside. I looked cute in my Sunday dress, and I didn't want it to get wet. It seemed as though there wasn't an umbrella big enough to shield me from the rain. Grandma Bean always made me go to church, no matter what. I could hear the music from outside. The drums were loud and thunderous.

I opened the door to see Linwood's dad, Mr. McDaniel, singing the Lord's Prayer. Mr. McDaniel could sing. Brandy and Shana were waving at me to sit beside them. Grandma Bean had all of us sitting on the pew where she could see us. I almost felt like a child. After Mr. McDaniel finished singing his song, Pastor Jacobs went up to preach. Pastor Jacobs was loud and ran all over the church. I just sat there and looked at everything that was going on. Occasionally, Shana would stand up and clap when people started shouting. Grandma Bean was always shouting while the ushers fanned her.

Grandma Bean said she couldn't help what the Holy Ghost was doing to her. She said if she was gonna shout, she was always gonna be real about it. One time she ran around the church so many times, she couldn't get out of bed the next morning because her legs were sore. She says one day I'll feel what she feels and understand. Soon it was time for the altar call.

Yep, it never failed. I looked back to see Linwood tiptoeing out the door. I knew he would leave like clockwork. Pastor Jacobs always asked everyone to close their eyes during the altar call, but I always liked to peak in order to see who came down. It wasn't too long before Rochelle was at the altar, crying hysterically, thanking Jesus for everything he had done for her. Everyone was fanning Rochelle while she was shouting thanks to the Lord.

"Nobody knows what God has done for me. God delivered me off them drugs! I sold my body and neglected my children. Thank you, Jesus! Thank you, Jesus!" Rochelle shouted. She went on and on about thanking God. I was genuinely happy for her. She seemed at peace with herself. I had never seen Rochelle show this church emotion about anything or anyone. Pastor Jacobs told everyone to keep Rochelle in prayer.

I went outside looking for Linwood, while Grandma Bean stayed inside to comfort Rochelle. Linwood was sitting in his father's car, smoking a cigarette. I went up to the car door and knocked to get his attention.

"What, girl? I'm handling business out here," he said.

Now, he wasn't trying to be funny.

"Oh, you not gonna let me in?" I said.

Linwood hesitated to open the door, but reluctantly let me in the car. I sat down. Secretly, I still had feelings for Linwood. Even though we'd never had sex, I felt bonded to Linwood.

"No, 'cause . . . ," he said.

"'Cause why?" I asked.

"Cause I don't want to," he replied. "Now leave me alone, girl, so I can finish smoking this piece before my dad comes."

"When did you start smoking?" I asked.

"Since I stopped going with you," he said.

Linwood smiled. He always knew how to make a girl feel special. I didn't want Linwood to know I still had feelings for him. So I pretended his comment didn't bother me.

"Did you steal those cigarettes?" I asked.

"Hell, no! Don't you know I'm on probation? I can't afford to get in trouble. Man, that's why I'm sick of this place!" he said.

"What place?" I asked.

Linwood looked at me as if I was crazy and replied, "This town and these people! When my probation is over, I'm gonna stay with my cousins down south. A black man ain't got no chance down here in the dumps."

"What about your dad? What's Mr. McDaniel gonna do without you here?" I asked.

"Live!" he said.

I myself didn't want Linwood to leave, nor had I ever thought he would. I thought he would be this thug who chased me forever. It concerned me that he had a plan. Oh, my God. Linwood had a plan?

"Well, *I* most certainly ain't never going nowhere!" I told him. "Unlike you, I can't leave my Grandma Bean by herself."

Linwood just looked at me, concerned.

"One day you won't have to leave here," he said. "She'll leave you. Grandma Bean is old."

"Shut the hell up, Linwood!" I shouted.

I was growing angry at the thought—of Grandma Bean raising me when my mama was locked up for murder, and not even knowing who my daddy was.

"So!" he said. "Everybody's life ain't great. You just have to deal with it!"

I couldn't believe Linwood was being so insensitive. I hurriedly got out of the car, almost tripping over my own two feet.

"This conversation is over, mister!" I said. I slammed the car door, leaving Linwood with a puzzled look on his face. Humph! I wasn't going to even think about that boy!

Chapter Thirteen

Pastor Jacobs came by the house to have dinner with us. Grandma Bean fried some fresh trout. I loved trout; it was my favorite fish. I don't know why, but I never liked freshwater fish; it had a different kind of taste. I always loved saltwater fish, and I loved me some fresh fried trout. It was yummy to my tummy!

As usual, Brandy had invited herself to dinner. I swear, that child didn't have any food at her home. Pastor Jacobs could eat a lot for a man his size. I could barely keep up with him. Of course, I like to have more fish than anyone else. There was only one person who could out-eat Pastor Jacobs, and that was Brandy. Pastor Jacobs was tall and muscular. I must admit he did kind of look like he used to be a drug dealer or a boxer in the past. I don't want to assume anything, but I bet he and Woody beat up a lot of people in their past. I watched Pastor Jacobs as he sucked the meat off the fish's bones. Brandy was just sitting doing nothing. Of course, Brandy had already finished her third helping of fish and had the "I'm stuffed" look on her face. Actually she looked miserable.

"Brandy, you know gluttony is a sin," I said.

I was just checking to see if Grandma Bean was paying attention to how much Brandy ate. Brandy looked disappointed and dropped her fork on her plate.

"Nope, I didn't know that," she replied.

Brandi then let out a sigh. I don't think she was too happy to find that out. Grandma Bean looked at me with a disappointed look. Then she popped me on my hand.

"You leave that baby alone, Micah," Grandma Bean said. "She eating for two now! A woman got to get all her nutrition she can so the baby can be good and healthy."

Brandy stuck out her tongue at me.

Pastor Jacobs cleared his throat and wiped the crumbs off his mouth and said, "Now, I didn't want to bring this up, but I think y'all should know. One of my old partners told me, Woody *is* back in town."

A sick, sinking feeling went straight to the pit of my stomach. Just the mention of his name had so much effect on me.

Grandma Bean gasped. She put her hands up against her head as if she didn't understand how this could be.

"Pastor, are you sure?" she asked.

It was as if Grandma Bean wanted him to say it wasn't true, or perhaps he'd made a mistake and said the wrong person was back in town. But I knew for sure. The devil don't bring no new tricks. Pastor sensed Grandma Bean's fear and discomfort.

"That's what I hear, Grandma Bean. But I wouldn't worry about him messing with y'all or nothing. He probably hiding out from the cops or something. People like Woody always in some kind of trouble."

I pushed my plate away from me. My stomach was so sick that I was trying to keep myself from throwing up. Pastor Jacobs knew

I was bothered by this news. He took my hand in his. Although he as a muscular man, he was also full of compassion.

"Listen to me, Micah," he said. "God did not give you a spirit of fear. Don't you ever fear Woody. Don't you ever give him any power over you. God will deal with him in time. You'll see. This I promise, Micah. This I promise!"

Somehow Pastor Jacobs' words were like little raindrops of healing to my soul. I really wanted to believe him. I really wanted to believe that Woody would be punished for what he'd done to Cherish. Woody led such a destructive life of crime. I was surprised no one had put out a hit on him from a gang or something. I was thinking of the many ways for Woody's life to end horribly, while Pastor Jacobs was lecturing me about God taking care of evil people. Pastor Jacobs noticed me staring in a deep space and decided to wrap up his little sermon to me.

"And that's why God has to take care of revenge for his people," he said. "Do you understand, Micah?"

I was so lost in emotion, I didn't think I even heard the last part of Pastor Jacobs' speech to me.

"Huh?" I said. "Oh, yeah, Pastor, I understand?"

In actuality, I wasn't tuned in to Pastor Jacobs, and he knew it.

"Micah, is you listening, child?" he asked.

I could see Pastor was determined to get my attention.

"Yeah, Pastor, I hear you," I replied. "I hear you loud and clear."

There was a loud knock at the door, and Grandma Bean rushed to answer it. I heard her talking to someone. She came into the kitchen with a beautiful woman. Everyone stopped talking and directed their attention to her. Grandma was smiling and hugging this woman who looked rich and sophisticated. Her perfume was enchanting and delightful. Her hands were French-manicured. She was a shapely woman with beautiful hair and curly eyelashes. Now, I have to admit, this woman looked good . . . damn good!

Grandma Bean was overly excited, hugging on the woman and everything, like she had known her forever or something.

"Guess who this is, y'all!" she said.

Grandma Bean urged the women to come closer in the kitchen. The woman reluctantly came toward us. I studied the woman's face. It was as if I had known her before or something. Just then, her face became clear to me. Pastor Jacobs and Brandy were still puzzled, though.

"Oh, my God! Rochelle is that you?" I asked.

My Lord, I just wanted to scream on the inside. I couldn't believe my eyes.

Rochelle smiled and let out a deep breath and replied, "It's me."

Pastor Jacobs started shouting and speaking in tongues. Rochelle looked beautiful. Rehab had done her well. I never knew that underneath all the drugs, cussing, and being mean was a beautiful woman waiting to come out. Grandma Bean was so happy to see Rochelle sober. She had always believed that Rochelle would beat the crack demon, that God would heal Rochelle. I guess now Rochelle believed that God had healed her too.

Chapter Fourteen

"Micah . . . telephone!"

It was Saturday morning, and boy was I sleepy and tired! I heard Grandma Bean calling my name, wanting me to pick up the telephone and answer the call. I pretended as though I didn't hear her calling for me. My body was just too tired to answer. I pretended I was still sleeping, but Grandma Bean was a very persistent woman.

"Micah! Telephone!" Grandma Bean shouted again.

I continued to ignore her. I just wanted to sleep late for a few more minutes. My eyes were heavy and kept closing as if they had a mind of their own. I heard Grandma Bean stomping up the steps.

"Micah! Do you hear me, child?" Grandma Bean yelled.

She came into the bedroom and stood directly over me. I could feel her breathing and panting heavily. I pretended to be sleep while ignoring her, hoping she would go away. Then I felt something hit my head! I felt a sudden rush of pain on the side of my head. I couldn't pretend to be asleep any longer after that. The pain was great. I let out a loud scream.

"Ouch!" I shouted. Grandma Bean had hit me over the head with the phone. "What did you do that for?"

She looked at me, gave me her fed-up look, and replied, "I knew you weren't asleep, you old scoundrel! That's what you get for trying to ignore your Grandma Bean! Now, lady, for the last time, you got a telephone call!"

Grandma Bean handed me the phone and stomped her way back downstairs. I still could not believe she had hit me with the phone. I didn't feel like talking, but I answered anyway.

"Hello?" I said.

"Hello, Micah. It's Mama, honey. I was just calling to see how you were doing. I'm just trying to keep up with ya. You never call me to talk or anything."

I wasn't mentally prepared to talk to Mama, especially *not* on an early Saturday morning!

"I've been busy doing other things," I replied. That was the best answer I could come up with. Mama was determined to carry on a conversation with me anyway.

"Yeah, I heard you were going to beauty school in the fall," she said.

I was surprised Mama knew about that. I really didn't want her to know anything about me. "How did you know I was going to beauty school?" I asked.

Initially, Mama was hesitant to answer. "A good mama should know everything about her child," she replied.

I paused for a minute. Was Mama implying she was a *good* mama? How dare she even suggest that she was a good mama? She had never even raised me, never even showed me how much she loved me. I just ignored her, because I didn't want to start arguing with her. Besides, my head still hurt from being hit with the phone.

"Mama, I really have to go right now," I said. "I need to get dressed for church. We're having revival this whole week, and you know how Grandma Bean loves being on time."

Mama let out a deep sigh and said, "I just pray God keeps your Grandma Bean happy and healthy. Hey, Micah, you look after my mama for me. Asa Lama Lakum!"

My mama must have lost her mind! She knew I didn't understand Spanish! "Mama, I don't know Spanish. Did you learn Spanish in prison?"

Mama giggled under her breath. "Honey, Asa Lama Lakum is from the Muslim faith. Allah has helped me deal with what I'm going through. Allah has helped me survive prison."

I was confused. I knew Grandma Bean had raised Mama in church. In fact, Mama used to usher in church. So why in the world wasn't she talking about how *God* had helped her to survive in prison? I was afraid ask Mama the most important question. The same question Cherish had asked me years ago.

"Mama, do you believe in God?" I asked.

There was silence on the phone. Then Mama let out a deep sigh.

"You know, at one time I *did* believe in your grandma's God. That was until I was sent to this hellhole they call prison. All that time your grandma had me going to church, praying to *her* God—for what? *Her* God didn't help me stop drinking all those years. *Her* God didn't send me no house. And most importantly *her* God didn't send me no husband! I believe *her* God was jealous of me when he found out that Woody was in my life.

109

Woody loved me! He wanted to marry me someday. Now all that can't ever happen because of *her* God! *Her* Christian God took all that away from me!"

I couldn't believe Mama was bold enough to talk about God like that! She was acting like it was his fault she was in jail! Even I had a certain level of fear of God!

"Look, I don't think we should be talking about God like this," I said. "Grandma Bean gets angry when you talk about the Father!"

Mama cleared her throat and replied, "I understand, Micah, but these are my beliefs, and I have a right to believe in whoever I want to believe in." I was disgusted at this point, and Mama knew it. "Well, let me go," she said. "My time is up. I hope you come and see me soon."

I hung the phone up slowly, thinking to myself that my mom was literally nuts! Then I said a quick prayer. "Lord please forgive my mama. She didn't mean to talk bad about you the way she did. She's just nuts!"

I heard Grandma Bean coming back upstairs. She came into the room and waited for me to say something in reference to the conversation I'd just had with Mama. I didn't say anything! I just pretended to be busy picking out clothes for the day. She came closer to me with her arms folded.

"Well?" she asked.

I know Grandma Bean wanted to know what me and Mama had talked about on the phone. After all, I had refused to talk to Mama up until that point. I avoided eye contact with Grandma Bean while picking out a shirt to go with my shorts.

"Well what?" I replied. I pretended to be completely puzzled as to what she was asking.

"What did you and Irish talk about?" she asked. "Did she say when she was gonna be getting paroled?"

I let out a big sigh.

"Mama just wanted to know how I was doing and stuff. All Mama said was she was proud that I was going to beauty school and making something of myself."

Grandma Bean paused for a second, as if she knew our conversation had been more in-depth than that.

"Well, that's good y'all talked and all," she said quickly. "I'm glad to see you have forgiven her."

I completely dropped my shorts out of my hand.

"I didn't say I forgive her!" I shouted. "I just talked to her for a while, that's all." Grandma Bean must have known she'd struck a nerve with that comment. By that time, I was under the bed trying to reach my tennis shoes. I didn't even realize that I had snapped at her. "I'm sorry I snapped, Grandma Bean," I said to her. "I just don't want to waste time talking about Mama. Besides why bother having a relationship with her when she will never be paroled?"

I could tell Grandma Bean was disappointed that I had not forgiven Mama. She turned to walk back downstairs before pausing once more.

"Well, baby, the world might say she'll never be paroled, but as long as your mama got God in her life, she'll walk right out of that jail cell one day." She proceeded to walk downstairs to the kitchen. I admired Grandma Bean's confidence in God. I didn't have the heart to tell her that Mama didn't even believe in *her* God anymore.

After breakfast I decided I would drop by Shana's house because I'd promised her I would do her hair. Shana had freshmen orientation at her college that week. She wanted to look good for the boys in the fraternities.

I was driving past Rochelle's house when I noticed her social worker dropping her and the kids off. Rochelle had developed a friendship with her social worker. Everybody was happy Rochelle was doing well at this point. She was staying clean from drugs and was allowed to have visits with her children on the weekends. She said they would come home for good soon.

I waved at Rochelle and her social worker. She looked real pretty and real happy! It's funny, when she was on drugs, I couldn't stand her mean self! Now that she was off drugs, I loved seeing her happy and blessed. Even Shelby, Rochelle's dog, looked happy and healthy. Like Grandma Bean always said, "God is good all the time, and all the time God is good!"

Shana was outside checking the mail when I pulled up her driveway.

"What's up, girl?" I said.

Shana was one skinny child! She reminded me of a white model or something. White people always complimented Shana on her figure, while black people worried if she was anorexic or something. She was torn on the inside. She didn't know whether to appreciate her figure or to be disgusted with it. Maybe that was why she cut all her hair off, to prove she was her own person. But I must admit, she could have been a model if she wanted to.

"Hey, Micah, girl, let's go in the house," she replied. "It is hot out here."

I followed Shana into the kitchen and began washing her hair. She always fidgeted when I washed her hair.

112

"Hold still, girl, so I can get this texturizer on your head!" I said.

"Hurry up, Micah," she said. "I'm hungry!"

Shana was driving me crazy! "Didn't you know you were hungry *before* I started putting this mess in your hair?" I asked.

"No. Now, hurry up!"

I finished putting the plastic cap on Shana's head.

"There! Now let it sit for a few minutes," I said. She made us some bologna sandwiches and sodas for lunch.

Shana had a beautiful house. She was kind of rich. Both her parents were bankers and drove fancy cars. Shana began fumbling through her music tapes.

"You want to hear some music?" she asked.

"Sure, okay. What kind?" I asked.

Shana smacked her lips as if she had the perfect song in mind. "Just listen, Micah," she said.

Shana fumbled through her tapes and then popped one into the stereo system. Out came some loud country music. Shana began dancing to the beat. I couldn't stand to see a rhythm-less black girl dance to country music.

"*Country music?*" I asked. Shana kept on dancing. It was horrible.

"Girl, are you crazy? When did you start listening to country music?" I asked.

She kept right on dancing. "Since I learned my ancestors were black cowboys. We black people are deeper than rhythm and blues or a side of hip-hop, ya know." She grabbed my hand, trying to make me dance with her.

"But why on earth are you listening to white folks' country music?" I asked. I could hardly catch my breath, trying to keep up with Shana. Finally she stopped dancing.

"Because, young lady, at one time your cowboys danced to it too. Why do you listen to rhythm and blues, hip-hop, or the blues? Black people have birthed all types of music for America. Plus, I just started liking country music."

I shrugged my shoulders. Truthfully I had no right or wrong answer for that. "Uh-huh. It doesn't sound that bad," I said. I began swaying my hips to the music. Country wasn't really that bad.

Shana and I were getting loud, laughing and dancing. I didn't want to disturb her parents. "We better calm down," I said. "I don't want to disturb your parents."

"Oh, girl, please!" she said. "They in Paris!"

"Paris?" I said.

"Yeah, they just wanted to get away for a while."

"And they left you here alone?" I asked.

"I am *grown*, you know!"

"Well, when they coming back?"

"Maybe Monday or Tuesday," she replied. "Mama just needs to do some shopping."

"Why didn't you go with your parents to Paris?" I asked.

"I don't want to go to Paris," she said. "I want to go to Africa."

"It's too hot over in Africa. Anyway, what you gonna do while they gone?" I asked.

"Girl, I don't know. You wanna stay over here and have a slumber party?"

"Girl, we too old for that now," I replied.

By that time, Shana and I had stopped dancing. We were both out of breath. Then Shana jumped up and down with excitement.

"I got it!" she said. "We can have a party."

"Great! I'll call Linwood, and he can get us a DJ. And we do want boys there, right?"

Shana smacked her lips and replied, "I know that's right! Make sure you tell Linwood to invite his cute friends."

"Yeah, some of Linwood's friends are ugly, and this ain't no Halloween party!" I said.

Shana and I burst out laughing. She hugged me.

"Girl, this is gonna be the best party of the year!" she said.

Chapter Fifteen

I told Grandma Bean I was sleeping over at Shana's house. I conveniently left out the part about having a party. Brandy decided to spend the night too. Brandy's aunt couldn't care less about anything she did.

By ten o'clock, Shana's house was crowded with all the kids from our school. The music was loud, and everybody was having a good time. Everyone was dancing, including Brandy. I didn't think Brandy would dance at the party, considering she was seven months pregnant. All I could see was Brandy's big belly moving up and down to the sound of the music. Linwood and I danced most of the night together. Linwood was a real good dancer. He knew all the latest dance moves. I must admit, Linwood was sexy. If I would have ever lost my virginity, I had hoped it would be with Linwood. Deep down, I knew Linwood had a good heart. We danced close on the slow songs. I felt as though we were the only people in the room. Our bodies were glued together like one big sin. Linwood began kissing on my neck. I was nervous and somewhat trembling. By that time, the music had changed to a hip-hop song. Everyone around us was dancing vigorously. Yet we were still slow-dancing. I looked up to see Linwood staring directly in my eyes.

"Micah, are we going to get married one day?" he asked.

I was stunned by this question. I opened my mouth hoping words would come out. I knew Linwood was waiting for an answer.

Before I could answer, Shana grabbed me by the hand, yelling hysterically. "Micah, come quick! It's Brandy, she's, she's . . ."

I could barely make out the words Shana was saying. She was hysterical. Brandy's eyes were rolling into the back of her head. Shana grabbed my hand and pulled me away from Linwood. She dragged me upstairs to her bedroom. I could barely keep up with her and almost tripped on the stairs. She flung open the bedroom door.

"Something's wrong with Brandy!" she shouted.

Brandy lay stretched out on the bed. She wasn't moving. The room smelled like marijuana. The only thing I could think was, *Lord, don't let another friend die on me!* Linwood burst through the bedroom door.

"What the hell happened?" he shouted.

I could tell Linwood was scared also. Shana looked at me as if I had an answer. My body was literally numb. This was the second friend I had found dead. I couldn't move my mouth.

Linwood pushed me out the way, looking for the telephone, only to find it on the other side of the room.

"Somebody call 9-1-1!" he shouted.

Shana obeyed Linwood's orders. Linwood ran over to Brandy to see if she was dead. Then he sighed with relief.

"It's okay," he said. "She's still breathing."

At 3:00 a.m., we were still at community hospital. Out of all those people who claimed to be our friends, only me, Shana, and Linwood had stayed with Brandy. Each one of us took our turns pacing the floor. I had never been so scared in my life. I had tried to call Brandy's aunt, but she wasn't at home, so I left her a message. Her sorry-tail aunt probably wouldn't come to the hospital anyway. That really showed how much she cared about Brandy.

Finally, the doctor came out and headed toward us. "I need to talk with her immediate family," he said.

I stood up quickly and said, "Yes, I'm Brandy's sister."

The doctor looked surprised and said, "Sister? I thought she had an aunt. Well, congratulations, it's a girl. Unfortunately, we had to call child protective services. The baby was born with crack cocaine in her system."

We all sat there stunned. I personally had mixed emotions. I was happy the baby was there, but I knew Brandy didn't do drugs. Shana looked at me as if she was waiting for me to explain the situation. The doctor left the room. There was so much tension in the air, you could cut it with a knife. Shana slid down the chair. I could tell she had reached her breaking point.

I felt like crap. What else could go wrong in my life? Brandy was lying up in the hospital with a new baby girl, born sick as hell. Shana was probably gonna get into a whole lot of trouble from her parents. Grandma Bean was gonna fuss me out. So much was running through my mind, I couldn't think straight. Shana began crying. Linwood just walked away, like he couldn't take it anymore. Linwood never could stand a woman crying. I went over to console Shana.

"Don't worry," I said. "Everything will be okay." My voice was trembling. Even I couldn't convince myself everything would be okay. Shana looked at me as if I was crazy for saying it.

"Are you nuts?" she asked. She began ranting frantically and said, "Our friend is lying up in the hospital with a crack baby. I don't even know how she got crack at the party. My mother and father will definitely kill me for this. I am in so much trouble!"

Shana was right. Everything was messed up. I had a nervous stomach and felt nauseated. "We'll get through this together, Shana," I said. "I'll go get us some coffee."

We didn't drink coffee—never touched the stuff—but keep in mind, we had been in the hospital all night. We needed something to keep us awake. Shana didn't object to it. I walked to the elevator, wondering how everything had just spiraled out of control so quickly. I was so tired. It had been a mentally and emotionally tiring night. It was all I could do to hold my head against the elevator.

Ding! Finally, the elevator opened. I was startled by a loud, screeching woman.

"Micah! What have you done?" Grandma Bean shouted.

Uh-oh! I'd spoken too soon. This was the one person I was not ready to face.

"Grandma Bean," I said, "let me explain!"

Chapter Sixteen

Grandma Bean hadn't spoken to me in over a week. She said she was so mad, she didn't know how to talk to me without sinning. Shana's parents wouldn't allow her to talk to me—especially since Brandy and the baby were now living with us. Brandy's aunt would not allow the baby in her home, and she didn't want the social worker coming there. Brandy got the same social worker as Rochelle.

Rochelle had been trying to talk to Brandy about not using drugs. Well, she needed to sweep around her own front door before she tried sweeping around Brandy's! Carmen had told me Rochelle was back using drugs. Besides, Brandy still didn't know how cocaine got in her system anyway. She didn't remember anything from that night. Linwood was very distant from us too. He didn't even talk to us in church anymore. He just sat in the back of the church with shades on. I swear, I don't know what he be thinking sometimes.

I could only watch Shana from the window, driving slowly down the street to go home. Sometimes she would sneak a peek at me as if to say, *I'm still thinking about you.* I always thought her parents felt they were better than everyone, sitting up in the church house all high and mighty. They acted like they too good to fan the sweat off their faces like the rest of us. I don't know what type of punishment Shana got, but for me, being apart from her was punishment enough. I could tell being apart from me was punishment for her too. Grandma Bean and I had been two strangers in the house for too long. It was time to talk.

I heard Grandma downstairs in the kitchen. I walked downstairs to where she was standing, doing what she did best—cooking.

"Dinner sure smells good," I said.

Grandma Bean let out a smile. "I'm glad you like it."

I wanted to continue the conversation. "What's for dinner?" I asked.

Grandma Bean let out a laugh, and replied, "Baby bottles! That reminds me y'all better order out tonight. I don't feel like cooking. It's been a long time since a baby has been in this house."

Grandma Bean looked stressed. All that time, I'd never thought about how this was affecting her. She was definitely getting older, and she had done her part in raising me already. Now it seemed like she was starting all over again. I ran upstairs and into Brandy's room.

Brandy was trying to feed the baby, but it seemed as though she was having a very hard time. She had a short temper. Even though it was supposed to be temporary, I knew she would be staying with us for a long time. "I can't get this baby to take my breast milk!" she said. "Micah, why the baby don't like my breast milk? Oh, my God, what if this ain't really my baby? What if they switched my baby at birth? You know, like they do on television shows."

Now, ordinarily one might think Brandy was kidding around, but judging by the puzzled look on her face, I knew she was serious. She just lay there looking at the baby with her breast halfway out and milk dripping from her nipple. At that point,

I was totally disgusted. "Can you please wipe up your dairy products?" I asked.

Obviously, Brandy had a delayed reaction to what I said to her. Realizing five minutes later that her big boob was sticking out in the open, she slowly started to cover herself.

"Oops, my bad," she said. "Sometimes I forget they there, girl. You know how it is."

"Um, no, I don't. My boobs are the size of acorns," I said.

I was trying to make Brandy laugh, but it didn't seem to be working. I could tell motherhood was something she was really worried about. "Brandy, you are not in this thing alone. We are all in this thing with you. We will all be in little Ariel's life!"

Brandy seemed pleased by this response and said, "I don't think I can do this alone, Micah. I mean, how am I supposed to be this child's mother when I never had a mother of my own? My mom ran out on me and left me with my evil aunt when I was a baby. Auntie already had three kids of her own, and she made it clear she didn't want any more kids in the house."

I had never asked Brandy how she wound up living with her aunt. I just knew she never talked about it, so I didn't either.

"I am so sorry, Brandy," I said. "I didn't know."

Brandy looked at me with a serious face and tears in her eyes. "How could you know?" she said. "You were always too busy wrapped up in your own sorrows. You hate your mom so much, you'd better be careful that you don't wind up just like her—like me!"

Now I was getting mad. How dare she say I'll wind up like my mom? I could feel my blood boiling. I paused briefly, throwing my hands up in the air. Lord, please give me strength not to cuss this girl out. Brandy knew she had struck a nerve by my body language. I spoke to her angrily.

"You know what? Don't say nothing to me no more, because I'm disgusted with you!"

Brandy tried to grab my hand. "Girl, I'm sorry!" she said.

I snatched my hand out of hers and walked off. Brandy knew I was mad. The one thing you don't do is compare me to Wild Irish Rose! The heffa better be glad I let her stay at my house!

The atmosphere became very awkward after my argument with Brandy. I was experiencing different feelings. Part of me didn't want Brandy there anymore, and I felt bad about those feelings. Hell, part of me didn't want to be there myself. Every day, I felt like leaving town. That party at Shana's had made me lose everyone I loved. I had lost Linwood and Shana. I think Linwood felt some type of responsibility for what happened to Brandy. After all, those were Linwood's friends he'd brought to the party. They were the ones responsible for slipping that cocaine into Brandy's drink, I'd heard. I couldn't talk to Shana about how I was feeling, because her parents would not allow us to have contact. Oh, how I missed them!

Chapter Seventeen

The hair dryer was hot! I don't know why black women block out their Saturdays to get their hair done. We endure the relaxers that leave their mark on our scalps, the hair rollers that breathe discomfort, and a block of time out of our lives—all to become beautiful for church on Sunday. Black women spend more on their hair than any part of their bodies. The pastor was telling folks, "Come as you are to the house of the Lord." I wonder, was he talking to black women? Grandma Bean had me sitting in Carmen's chair every two weeks for as long as I can remember. That's probably why my hair is so long now. Grandma Bean valued long hair. She used to say, "A woman's hair is her crowning glory." It was hot in this salon, but it did give me the chance to get away from Brandy.

A week had gone by and I still hadn't talked to her. She had really pissed me off! After all I had done for her, you'd think she'd be grateful! I had to put her out of my mind. I only had four weeks until beauty school started. I'm the type of person who can only focus on one thing at a time. I could already do hair; I just needed a license. To tell you the truth, I could do hair better than Carmen. Every hairstyle she put on my head, I did on Brandy's hair—and her hair is nappy!

"Carmen, when I get my license, you gonna let me work in your salon?" I asked her.

Carmen looked surprised. She looked at me while placing her hand on her lip. "Honey, I didn't know you wanted to work for me. I could have given you a job as a shampoo girl."

"A shampoo girl? You mean I can work here without my license?"

"Child, please! That's how I started out," she said.

I was so excited. I was one step closer to my dream. Who knew it would be this quick? I could see myself owning my own beauty salon, making my own hours, being my own boss. I don't think God made me to work a regular nine-to-five job. Finally, something was going right in my life!

"When do I start?" I asked.

Carmen let out a sigh. "Well, I guess you could start tomorrow. Bright and early. I got an 8:30 a.m. appointment."

"I'll be here at 8:00!" I said.

I couldn't wait to go home and tell Grandma Bean and Brandy the good news. Oh, wait. I would just tell Grandma Bean, because I was still mad at Brandy!

I was driving home fast. I couldn't wait to tell Grandma Bean. As I got closer to the house, I could see Brandy on the porch, shucking corn. I slowly got out of the car, wondering in my mind what to say to Brandy. It's funny because I had never intended on becoming Brandy's friend. It's funny how she wound up living there, as if we needed someone else in the house *and* a baby! Sometimes I don't know what God be thinking. I slammed the car door shut and slowly walked up the stairs to the porch.

"You know, you really shouldn't have that baby out here in this hot sun," I said.

125

Brandy looked at me with a surprised look on her face. Sometimes she could be so dumbfounded. She hesitated before responding. "I was finishing up this corn to take over to Rochelle. You wanna help? You supposed to be doing this anyway."

"Says who?" I asked.

"Says Grandma Bean, but you was off beautifying yourself at Carmen's."

I couldn't argue with that. Knowing Grandma Bean, Brandy was telling the truth on that one. She stopped shucking corn and looked directly at me.

"Well?" she said.

I repositioned myself and cleared my throat. I knew it was coming. Brandy was expecting an apology. I stood there with my hand over my hip. Brandy looked me dead in my eyes. Both of us were classified as stubborn women. This showdown could go on all night. I held my position steady in the red-hot sun for an additional twenty minutes. By that time, sweat was dripping down my face. My beautiful sundress was glued to my body.

"All right, you win! I'm sorry!" I raised up my hands as if to say, *I give up.*

Brandy let out a silent chuckle. Then she went back to shucking corn. "I knew you would give in sooner or later," she said. "Things didn't have to go this far. You could have just accepted my apology in the beginning, but nooo! You had to try and make a sister beg for forgiveness!"

Brandy was right. Inside, I wanted her to pay for hurting my feelings. I didn't understand how to let stuff go. I guess I was so used to not forgiving my mom, I never learned how to forgive others. I wasn't good at taking people back into my life after

126

they had hurt me. Maybe it was time I started. I held my head down in shame. I knew she was waiting for me to say something, but I couldn't say anything.

"Micah, we shouldn't let things come between us. We should have a relationship that's stronger than that. Your grandmother opened her home to me. Where would I be without her? I think of her as my own grandmother. I would like to think of you as my sister."

Brandy was irritating me, partly because I knew she was right. Of course, I was never going to admit she was right. I had already apologized, and in my book, that was enough. Grandma Bean came bursting through the door, wearing her old housecoat and run-down slippers.

"Brandy, you'd better get that baby out of this hot weather," she said. "It's too hot for a baby to be out on the porch."

"Yes, ma'am!" she said. Brandy would never argue with Grandma Bean about parenting. Brandy took little Ariel inside as Grandma Bean had told her to. You know, it was funny. How in the world could Brandy do everything Grandma Bean said except keep from naming that child after a mermaid?

And in all the excitement, I'd forgotten to tell Grandma Bean about my new job.

Chapter Eighteen

The church house was rocking with Spirit-filled church music. It was getting hot in there! My church dress was starting to cling to my body from the sweat. The air conditioning was running, but there were so many people shouting and running around the church, the air couldn't circulate. I had to excuse myself and go get some air. I slid by Grandma Bean in order to make my way to the aisle. She pulled on my dress as if to get my attention.

"Don't get dirty," she said. "We going to see ya mama after this."

Oh, great. Just what I needed—a visit to see my mom. "Oh, all right, Grandma Bean, I won't get dirty," I said.

I made my way down the church aisle and burst through the door. Ah . . . fresh air. I walked around the church a little bit to dry out my new dress. I walked through the parking lot, only to see Linwood sitting in his dad's car, puffing on a cigarette. He looked like an old Mac Daddy! He looked like he didn't want to be bothered, but I went over to talk with him anyway. I came by the driver's side window.

"Hey, why you out here instead of inside church?" I asked. Linwood looked kind of depressed. His eyes seemed watery, and he wouldn't look at me. I decided to cheer him up by playing with him. "Hey, big-head, you didn't have to look so down, ya know?"

Linwood's nostrils flared up. "God, Micah, can't you see I want to be alone right now?" he shouted.

No, he *didn't* raise his voice at me. "Dang!" I said. "Sorry for trying to cheer you up!"

I gave him the hand and turned around and marched back up the church steps. I flopped down beside Grandma Bean. She looked at me as if I had lost my mind. Then she leaned over to me and whispered, "Quiet, girl. Pastor's about to do the call to altar."

Pastor began by asking everyone to bow their heads and pray for the lost souls. I bowed my head, but I couldn't think of anything. I was too hungry to pray. Church always made me hungry. I could hear the Pastor continuing to speak with authority.

"God can forgive anything you did," he said. "Won't you give God a chance to be your lawyer, doctor, healer, and most importantly, your comforter? Why don't you give it all to God?"

Pastor Jacobs continued speaking. I thought about everything I had been through. The Pastor spoke on. "Oh, why won't you come lay your burdens down at the altar? You have nothing to lose."

I always thought I would wait until I got married to be holy. That way it would look good. I felt a knot in my throat like I could cry. I could hear Grandma Bean praying quietly, and I wondered if she was praying for me. I didn't want to cry. I kept telling myself, *Hold it in, Micah, hold it in!*

"Come, come to the altar and bow down and worship him with your whole heart and soul," Pastor Jacobs said.

I heard footsteps coming toward me. They stopped at my pew. I tried to peak without being noticed. I saw baggy jeans and white tennis shoes with dirt on the back. Whoever this person was, he reeked of cigarette smell. It looked as though drops of water were falling on his shoes. One drop after another began to slide down his white shoes. The footsteps began slowly walking down the aisle. I lifted my head a little until I could see the person's knees shaking nervously. I didn't know when to lift up my head so I kept it down.

Suddenly I heard thunderous applause. I felt the pew become lightweight. I realized I was the only one sitting down. I stood up to see who it was. It was Linwood! Linwood was standing at the altar with his hands raised, saying, "God, I surrender" over and over again. His face was down in tears. I started to cry too. I was in awe of what I had seen. I couldn't believe Linwood had gotten saved!

As he stood there in his street clothes, he looked far from holy. I just couldn't believe Linwood got saved. I mean, I would have imagined *myself* being saved before Linwood. Linwood's father came down out of the choir stand to comfort Linwood. I could see Shana in the front pew beside her parents, crying. She looked back at me as if to agree in disbelief that Linwood got saved. I gave her a smile back as if to say, *I know.*

Shana's mother quietly tapped Shana on the arm for her to turn around, once she realized Shana was making contact with me. I don't think that woman will ever give me back my best friend. Shana reluctantly obeyed her mother. Dang! Shana's Mama acted like I'd murdered somebody or something!

A group of men surrounded Linwood and hugged on him. Linwood's father was very emotional and crying. I never seen a grown man cry so much. I just sat in disbelief, wondering what had made Linwood get saved. What was going through his mind as he walked down the aisle? I mean, I had just been talking to him outside. He showed no signs of wanting to get closer to God just a few minutes ago. I was in disbelief. Church adjourned, and I was still sitting there wondering what had happened while he was sitting in the car outside. Unbelievable! In a matter of minutes, he went from sinner to saved!

Chapter Nineteen

Grandma Bean kept boasting at dinner about Linwood getting saved. Brandy found it fascinating. I excused myself early from the table. No one realized that I started my new job at Carmen's tomorrow. I'd never had a chance to tell Grandma Bean or Brandy. I didn't understand what all the hype was about? Cherish was saved, and she died early—real early. I mean, being saved didn't keep you from dying. Look at Rochelle. How many times was she gonna get saved? That girl done got saved enough for five or six peoples' souls. I been to church all my life, and all I see is people trying to get in good with the Lord and praying to him for money!

I retreated upstairs to my room. I just wanted some peace and quiet for once—without Brandy. I had my clothes laid out for my big day at work the next morning. It wasn't five minutes before Brandy came knocking on my door. She always did have bad timing.

"Micah, telephone! It's Linwood!" Grandma Bean shouted up just as Brandy barged her way through the door and looked around the room.

I told Grandma to hold on before I got the phone. "Can I help you?" I asked Brandy.

"Why you got your clothes laid out?" she asked. "Where you going?"

Finally, somebody wanted to know what was going on in my life. "If you must know," I said, "I start my new job tomorrow."

Brandy placed her hand on her hip. "Ha! You ain't got no job."

"I start my new job at Carmen's tomorrow, washing hair," I said. "See how much you know."

Brandy handed me the telephone, still in disbelief.

"I'm gonna tell Grandma Bean," she said.

"Fine, go ahead," I said. "You're doing me a favor."

I grabbed the phone and waved my hand, instructing her to leave the room. I lay across my bed. I wanted to get into the most comfortable position to hear all Linwood's gossip—like why he was trying to impress his dad by getting saved.

"What's up, Linny?"

"Hey, I just was calling . . . uh . . . uh."

If Linwood was hesitating to tell me something, it must be bad.

"Well, spit it out!" I said.

"I'm moving to Memphis with my aunt Pat," he said.

My heart dropped. I had a sinking feeling in my stomach. "Are you for real?" I asked. "Why are you moving? When are you moving?"

"I got to get out of North Carolina, period!" he said. "My life ain't been right since Mama died. Aunt Pat and Uncle Bobby married. Dad thinks it's a good idea to move where I can have two parents looking after me. He said he gonna move down at the end of the month. He sending me on the bus tomorrow. Aunt Pat and Uncle Bobby real excited for me to come."

"So that's it," I said. "You just gonna leave? Is that why you pretended to get saved, so your aunt and uncle would want you?"

"Now, hold on, Micah. I got saved for real!"

I interrupted him. "You 'bout as saved as Rochelle is!" I shouted.

"Don't you judge me, girl! You the one need to be saved, as good as Cherish was to you," he said.

"How dare you bring Cherish into this, boy!" I shouted.

"Look, Micah, you shouldn't question my religion. You need to get yourself right. Look at everything that's happened to you. You might as well believe in something. We supposed to be like, you know, close and all, so I thought I should tell you good-bye. You are kind of like my girl and all. I'm leaving tomorrow, and if you want to see me off, then you can. If you don't, then I'll just have to go on through life without you; but somehow I always imagined you in it. Look, I gotta go. I need to finish packing before my dad gets home. Just think about what I said. Hopefully, I'll see you tomorrow, okay?"

I hesitated in responding to him. Somehow I knew this would be the last time I talked to him, and I just wanted to hear him talk so I could bring it into remembrance when I thought of him.

"Okay, Linwood."

Chapter Twenty

I never officially said good-bye to Linwood. He didn't even call me to say good-bye. I was depressed, knowing he would be so far away from me. I'd always thought he would be there for me, but now I guessed he wouldn't. I buried my head under the covers, quietly sobbing. I would rather suffer in silence than let anyone know I was crying over Linwood. The truth was, Linwood really liked me, and it felt good to be liked. I lay in bed, wondering what my life would be like without Linwood.

I never heard from Linwood, although he invaded my mind once in a while. I really had never imagined my life without Linwood. He was the one person I could count on. I didn't want to grow old without him. I guess I took him for granted, just figuring he would always be there. He hadn't even called me. That was surprising, considering he'd always called me every day.

Days turned into months and months turned into years. Yet one thing remained the same, and that was my friendship with Brandy and Shana, which flourished over the years. We were like the three divas. Brandy tried moving back in with her aunt, but they would only get in constant arguments when Ariel would cry and get on her aunt's nerves. Then Brandy would show up at our door with Ariel. Grandma Bean would welcome her back and feed her and put her to bed. Brandy always said that sometimes family could bring you down. She was right; family *could* bring you down.

My life was *so* routine right about then. I mean, I thought I was in a rut. Every day it was the same old thing. It seemed as though everyone else had moved on with their lives. Shana had gone to school; Brandy had Ariel. I'd been working at Carmen's for a while, and I needed a vacation. Brandy came in with the cordless phone, shouting in my ear while holding onto poor Ariel.

"It's Shana!" she said.

"Okay, I got it," I said.

Brandy didn't hang up the phone. "Um, I think Shana called to speak to me," she said.

I held the phone to my ear.

"I called to speak to both of you," Shana said.

Of course, I had to roll my eyes at Brandy and turn my attention back toward the phone.

"What's up, girl?" I said excitedly. "It's good to hear from you!"

"What's up, my peoples?" Shana said. "I was calling to invite you all to homecoming this weekend. You all can stay in the room. My roommate is going home that weekend."

Before I could answer, Brandy blurted out, "Yes! We'll be there!"

I was tired of Brandy being in every aspect of my life. She was like a cancer that was taking over.

"Uh, Brandy, don't you have to check with your social worker before taking that baby out of town?" I asked.

Shana gasped on the other end of the phone. "Ooh, Brandy, they gonna take your kid like they did Rochelle's?" she asked.

Brandy was growing angry with me for bringing that up.

"Now, they ain't gonna take my kid. My social worker just needs to know I ain't left town with Ariel. Grandma Bean can keep her while I go."

"Hell, no, she ain't!" I replied. I was tired of Brandy convincing my grandma to do for her. Besides, here lately, Grandma Bean had been off and on sick with the flu bug. She'd been real weak and even lost more weight.

"I mean, Brandy, why can't you just take care of your responsibilities?" I asked.

"I take care of my responsibilities," she said. "I'll just ask Grandma Bean to take care of Ariel. You best believe I'm going on that trip!"

"Not if I can help it!" I said.

An argument was brewing. Shana interrupted.

"Look, just talk to Grandma Bean about it, okay?" Shana said.

We both looked at each other as if we knew what Grandma Bean was going to say. I had a smile on my face, knowing in my heart that she would take my side. She knew I needed a break from here. Brandy looked a little worried.

"Look, I gotta go," Shana said. "Love you guys. Tell you me what you decide."

"All right. Peace!" Brandy and I shouted.

Of course, Grandma Bean said yes . . . to Brandy, that is. I couldn't believe I was stuck with going to town with this woman. The only good thing that came out of this was that Grandma Bean let us drive her car. Still, my life was in a rut, and I needed a break. I thought getting out of town would be just what I needed. I picked up the phone and dialed Shana's number.

"Speak," Shana said.

"Is that the way you answer the phone?" I asked.

"Oh, what's up, Micah?"

"Just calling to tell you we are coming this weekend." I could hear the excitement in Shana's voice. I smiled to myself. You know what? It was about to be on!

Chapter Twenty-One

I could not believe what I saw on that beautiful college campus. Shana played our tour guide throughout this African paradise. She took pride in knowing she attended a historically black college. Shana walked as if this was her land, and she was proud of it. I saw black Greek fraternities stepping, and the band was marching throughout the yard. You could hear the sound of well-trained musicians jamming to the seventies soul music.

Brandy enjoyed this by constantly stopping and dancing. Shana and I would join in from time to time. Brandy sure could dance. Shana and I just irritated her. I was in awe that there were so many different shades of color. There were light-skinned, dark-skinned, brown-skinned, and some white people there. There were so many shades of me. There were so many shades of my people. It was at that moment that I envied Shana. To have an opportunity to learn about your career and your heritage was priceless. Shana led us through a crowd down by the cafeteria. Shana reported that this was the "strip."

Shana pointed to a couple of guys as if to classify them and said, "He's rich; he's riding on a loan check—that's not even his car."

"Wait! Wait, Shana." Brandy interrupted her as if she just didn't understand.

"What does "riding on a loan check" mean?" she asked.

It means, missy, that they'll pay it back later," Shana replied.

We all laughed. Who would want to get in that much debt just to impress people? We were all having a good time. The music was pumping. It was a relaxing atmosphere—until I saw him. And he saw me from behind his cigar, behind his shame, behind his wicked smile, and most of all, behind his guilt. I couldn't believe it! I couldn't believe that Woody was there!

I couldn't move. I couldn't believe he was sitting there like he ain't done nothing, smoking his cigar. Shana bumped into me, not realizing I had stopped walking, and Brandy bumped into her.

"Girl, what's wrong with you?" Shana asked.

I heard Shana talking to me, but I couldn't move. All this time had gone by, and this coward had never showed his face—not at Mama's trial, not at Cherish's funeral, not anywhere! I placed my hand on Shana's face and turned it toward Woody and his gang.

"Oh, my God!" she shouted.

The disbelief was all over Shana's face. Brandy was also noticing Woody. He noticed us and smiled a wicked smile. Then he and his gang came walking toward us. Woody stopped in front of me. He was standing so close to me, he could have kissed me. The stench of his guilt, horrible cigar, and breath sickened my stomach.

"Well, well, well. Long time, no see, Ms. Micah," he said.

I ignored him, thinking that this murderer could not be talking to me. Even though Woody wasn't in jail for murdering Cherish, I knew he had murdered her. Woody became annoyed that I was ignoring him. He grabbed my arm and yanked it furiously.

"You'd better listen to me when I'm talking to you, girl!" he shouted.

I gave him a serious look, like he didn't scare me one bit. "Don't you touch me, boy!" I replied. I jerked my arm back as if I was disgusted by his presence. I could tell this made him very angry. He lunged at me as if he was going to hit me. Brandy and Shana jumped back, but I knew the demon I was dealing with. If he were to hit me, I was prepared to hit him back. He saw me drawing up my fist. He was surprised at this.

"Oh, you gonna hit me now?" he asked.

"If you touch me again, I will hit you," I said.

I stood my ground. I was definitely not moving anywhere. A smirk appeared on Woody's face. Shana and Brandy grabbed my arm to shake it away from him. This upset Woody in a major way. His smile turned into a snarl.

"I like feisty women. Ya girl Cherish was a feisty woman," he said.

It was then I raised my fist and punched him in the face . . . and that was how we landed in jail.

Grandma Bean bailed us out of jail the next morning. Now I knew how Mama must have felt, sitting behind bars. I took the blame; being charged with assault wasn't the highlight of my life. I really didn't want any of it on Shana's record. She would have gotten kicked out of school for sure. Brandy was too scared to fess up to anything. It really didn't matter. The truth was the truth. I hit him, so I should be charged. Times like this, I could talk with Linwood. Only Linwood wasn't around.

Now I was sitting at the breakfast table looking at Grandma Bean. Oh, no, here it came—one of Grandma Bean's speeches.

"What were you thinking, hitting Woody like that?" she shouted. "You know that man is dangerous!"

I concentrated on eating my cereal. Still in a daze while eating slowly, I could just see Woody's face and that sneaky smile. It made my stomach turn. At least I wasn't like Mama, and I didn't let him run over me. When I hit him, I realized then that he wasn't invincible. He was human. Grandma Bean awaited my reply. I put down my spoon and laid it in my cereal.

"Well, what do you have to say for yourself?" she shouted. "Micah, I'm talking to you! You hit a monster!"

"He's just a man," I shouted back. "I got to get to work at Carmen's."

I excused myself and headed out the door. As I was heading out, Brandy' social worker, Ms. Williams, was about to knock at the door. She darted out of my way just in time. I yelled back at her, "Brandy's inside. Enter at your own risk!"

As I left for work, it began pouring down rain. The thunder was so loud, the car was shaking. I wasn't supposed to do it. I'd promised I wouldn't do it, but I had to go see Mama again. I sped off in the rain. The only thing I could think about was telling Mama that I'd stood up to her sorry man. I had done what she couldn't do.

Forty-five minutes later, I arrived at the prison. By that time, my blood was boiling. I was mad. I anxiously scurried through all the security checks. My cell phone kept ringing. It was Carmen, trying to get through. I really wasn't thinking about my new job or my responsibilities. When they brought Mama in, she seemed excited to see me. She went to hug me, and I immediately drew back. She sat down, eager to talk to me.

"Hey, baby, this is a surprise, but I'm glad you came to see me today," she said.

I interrupted her very quickly. "Mama, I saw Woody."

Mama's mouth dropped open. She appeared to be in disbelief. All of a sudden, a smirk appeared on her face. Then she said the words that would tick me off forever.

"Did he ask about me?" she said excitedly.

I could not believe she asked me that! "Did he ask about you?" I said. "No, he didn't ask about you. He hasn't come to see you since you been in here. Why would he ask about someone as pathetic as you?"

"Now hold up! I'm still your mother. As long as I live, you will respect me."

"As far as I'm concerned, you're not my mother," I said. "Grandma Bean is my mother. And as long as she lives, I will respect her."

Mama stood up above and looked me in the eye. "Well, then, I guess you got about six more months of respect left," she said.

"What do you mean?" I asked. "What's wrong with Grandma Bean?"

"She didn't tell you? Why don't you ask *your mama!*"

Mama called for the guard, and he took her away. All the while, Mama had a smirk on her face.

Suddenly I had a horrible feeling in the pit of my stomach that something was terribly wrong. Mama knew that the only thing that would tear my spirit down was if something happened to Grandma Bean. I needed to get home. I drove home so fast, I was surprised no cop stopped me. I pulled up to the driveway and screeched on the brakes, ran up the stairs and flung open the front door.

There was Grandma Bean and Brandy in the living room. Grandma Bean had her arm around Brandy with one hand and the phone to her ear with the other. Brandy's eyes appeared swollen. She looked like she'd been crying. I heard Grandma Bean tell the person on the other end of the phone. "Okay, she's here now."

Grandma Bean slowly put down the phone. I knew this wasn't good. I sat down in the chair.

"Micah, that was your mama on the phone. I know what she told you."

Somehow Mama had managed to call Grandma Bean before I got back home. "Well, Grandma Bean, what's wrong with you?" I asked hesitantly.

At that point, Brandy ran upstairs, crying and yelling, "I just can't believe it!"

I had never seen Brandy cry like that, not even when her family deserted her.

"Micah, I have cancer, and it's spread throughout my body. The doctor gave me six more months at the most. It's terminal; there's no need for any treatment. Your mom has known about it for some time now. I was going to tell you. I just didn't know how."

I felt numb all over my body. I couldn't cry or nothing. It was like an out-of-body experience. My life was essentially over.

Chapter Twenty-Two

The next couple of months were hard for me and Brandy. Poor little Ariel had no idea what was going on. Ironically, I spent more time with Ariel than Brandy did. Neither one of us could bear to see Grandma Bean going through her battle with cancer. I took time off cosmetology school so I could spend as much time with Grandma Bean as possible. What do you say to someone who is dying? Grandma Bean acted as if nothing was wrong.

Daily, she went about her routine as if her frail body had forever to live. Pastor Jacobs came by to see Grandma Bean every day, constantly praying for her. I stopped working for Carmen—temporarily, of course. I definitely wanted to make the most of the time we had left. I avoided Mama as much as possible. Part of me wondered if she'd meant any of this to happen to Grandma Bean. Then other times I would hear her crying on the telephone. Sometimes I would listen in on her phone calls.

Today I was supposed to be relaxing on the couch by myself. Ariel was finally asleep. She really wasn't sleeping through the night. All of a sudden, I heard a car honking the horn. It was Brandy's social worker. I wondered what she wanted.

"Hey, Ms. Williams, how are you? Come on in." Ms. Williams came in while inspecting the place closely with her eyes. She was a young social worker and seemed like she was fresh out of school. And boy, did she seemed stressed!

"Is everything all right today?" I asked.

"You're the fourth home visit I been on today," she said.

"I sure would not want your job!" I told Ms. Williams while patting Ariel's back.

"Not many people do!" she said.

Ms. Williams watched me while I comforted Ariel, trying to get her to fall asleep.

"That might as well be your baby!" Ms. Williams said with a smile.

I smiled back, holding Ariel close to me. "This *is* my baby!" I said.

"No, it ain't!" Brandy came flying down the stairs with a disturbed look on her face. "You didn't give birth to her."

I was just about to tell her a piece of my mind, when Ms. Williams butted in and asked,
"So, Brandy, how many parenting classes do you have left?"

Brandy sat down on the couch beside Ms. Williams and replied, "Oh, about that. I have to repeat the class, because Grandma Bean is dying of cancer."

"Oh, my God!" Ms. Williams shouted and then gasped for air.

I couldn't believe Brandy had just blurted it out so matter-of-fact. Ms. Williams looked as though she was going to cry. Brandy was so insensitive and immature. It would be a wonder if she was ever responsible enough to raise a child.

"Is she taking chemotherapy or anything?" Ms. Williams asked.

Ms. Williams wanted answers, and she wasn't playing. It was difficult for me to discuss Grandma's prognosis, but someone responsible had to.

"No, Ms. Williams. It started as brain cancer, and it's terminal. The cancer has spread throughout her body.

Ms. Williams gasped for air before getting up. Brandy had a way of putting her foot in her mouth and now looked dumbfounded, as if she had no idea why Ms. Williams retreated upstairs to see Grandma Bean. I looked at Brandy as if she had to be the dumbest animal on the planet! Brandy looked at me before shrugging her shoulders.

"What?" she said.

"You know what!" I said back to her.

"I mean, what did I say, Micah?" she asked.

"Brandy, did it not occur to you that the only reason she allowed Ariel to stay with you is because of Grandma Bean? Now you may have jeopardized Ariel's placement." I grabbed Ariel and headed upstairs. I swear, sometimes that girl really gets on my nerves.

We had been upstairs for a few minutes when Brandy came upstairs and busted through the door. It startled me and woke up Ariel. "Girl, what is your problem? Now you woke up the baby?" At that point, I was furious!

Brandy grabbed Ariel out of my arms. "This here is *my* baby! You need to have your own!" she shouted.

I couldn't believe she was talking to me this way. After all I had done to help that girl!

I grabbed Ariel back out of her arms and dared Brandy to take her back. Brandy just folded her arms and stood there. "Look, Brandy! I just don't want child services to take her away. The only reason they let you keep Ariel is 'cause she's in Grandma Bean's house. What do you think will happen when Grandma Bean has passed on? You ain't halfway going through your classes. You always making up excuses as to why you not going to them. When are you gonna grow up and take some responsibility?" Brandy stormed out of the room, leaving Ariel and myself.

A few minutes later, I heard Brandy scream. "Call 9-1-1! It's Grandma Bean!"

I ran into Grandma Bean's room, only to see Brandy holding Grandma Bean's lifeless body and Ms. Williams on the phone yelling, "We need an ambulance!" I couldn't believe it! I just stood there frozen in time. I couldn't believe my eyes. Could Grandma Bean be dead?

Chapter Twenty-Three

By the time they took Grandma Bean to the hospital, she was unconscious. She was being kept in the intensive care unit. Brandy, Ariel, and I stayed with her in the hospital. She looked so lifeless. Brandy remained outside the room, while I went to be by Grandma Bean's side. This disease had literally diminished Grandma Bean's body. The only thing alive was her spirit.

"Grandma Bean, can you hear me?" I whispered.

Grandma Bean slowly lifted her head and looked toward me. "Of course, I can hear you! I ain't dead yet!"

Tears flowed from my eyes. I was relieved to hear her voice.

"Grandma Bean, please don't die!" I said.

"Now look here! It's not up to you whether or not I live or die. It's up to God. God has the last say-so. God and God only! Don't cry for me if I die before you. You should be jealous that I get to see God before you do! God's timing is his timing, and when he says our time is up, it's up!"

"But Grandma Bean, what am I suppose to do without you?" I asked. "How am I supposed to live? You were my mother and my father. No one can replace that."

Grandma Bean's eyes welled up with tears. Then she held up her head proudly. "God has used me to take care of you," she said. "I believe I have done what God asked me to do. Now *you* need to do whatever God asks you to do."

I was puzzled. How could I talk about duties when my grandmother was dying?

"Grandma Bean, I have so much that I want, that I need. I mean, I need help with Ariel. Brandy's no good. I need a mother. I need a best friend. I need unconditional love. I need a family of my own. I need you, Grandma Bean. That's why you can't die!"

I was so emotional, I was choking on every word.

"Micah, God is all you need. And once you figure that out, everything you need and desire will be added to you. Listen to me!" she pleaded. "Take care of Ariel and Brandy. Those girls came into your life for a reason."

Grandma appeared very weak, so I didn't want to keep her talking. Her eyes closed, and she drifted off to sleep. Brandy walked back into the room.

"Is everything all right, Micah?" she asked.

I glanced over at Grandma Bean. For the first time, she looked at peace since being diagnosed with cancer. Since she was at peace, I was at peace.

I slept hard that night. I awoke the next morning to find everyone in the room extremely quiet. Brandy and Ariel were fast asleep. I went over to check on Grandma Bean. I noticed that the machine monitors were unplugged. Grandma Bean lay in the bed with her eyes open. It was then that I realized she was gone. Grandma Bean had gone on to be with the Lord.

The day of the funeral was a beautiful day. The sky was so blue. Grandma Bean had requested in her will that we all wear white. Have you ever been so numb that emotionally you remove yourself from an event? That's how I felt. They had the nerve to bring Mama to the funeral dressed in shackles and a prison uniform. We didn't speak two words to each other. I couldn't help feeling that I wanted my mom and Grandma Bean to exchange places.

The only thing I really remember is Brandy holding my hand and squeezing it tight. Shana rubbed my back. Nothing made me feel better. Actually, I just couldn't feel anything.

The next thing I knew, I was in my grandmother's bed, along with Shana, Ariel, and Brandy. What could anyone say? I had lost two people in my life who had meant so much to me. I didn't understand God sometimes. The good people in my life had died, and the bad people like Mama were still there.

We all lay in Grandma Bean's bed together, not knowing what to say. Brandy kept moving and switching sides. I knew she wanted to talk about something. Shana and I tried to work it out, but after a couple more twists and turns, I couldn't take it anymore. "What is it Brandy?" I asked.

Brandy looked at us with that "who, me?" look. "Oh, I wasn't trying to bother nobody. I was just thinking about Grandma Bean."

Before I could speak, Shana butted in and said, "Uh, duh . . . we're all thinking about Grandma Bean."

Brandy abruptly stood up as if she was about to give a speech and replied, "No, that's not what I'm saying. I mean, what are we supposed to do without Grandma Bean? She is the very thing that held this family together."

Brandy began to cry. We all were hurting. I guess I never thought Grandma Bean would die before I did. It wasn't supposed to be that way. What was God doing, taking away good people like Grandma Bean and Cherish? Didn't he know we needed them on earth more than he needed them in heaven? God was selfish! And from that day on, that was the way I would look at it!

Chapter Twenty-Four

Six months had passed since Grandma Bean's death. Brandy and I had decided to stay in the house we were raised in. Grandma Bean had left me the money to take care of both of us, including Ariel. The house was paid for, so we only had to worry about the utilities and taxes. Brandy finished her parenting classes, and Ms. Williams closed her child welfare case on Brandy.

Rochelle found herself in and out of rehab, trying to stay away from that "white devil," as she called it. I heard some of her kids were adopted out. The younger kids were supposed to be the ones that got adopted. It was hard to get the older children adopted, 'cause everybody wants younger kids. From time to time, I would hear Rochelle fussing about her kids.

I was still working at Carmen's while going to school part-time. Brandy had thought about going into the military. She was scheduled to see the recruiter at 2:00 p.m. today. Brandy was busy cleaning up the house, while I was taking care of Ariel. I'd never seen Brandy so nervous about anything in her life. She was definitely interested in going into the military. She'd even picked out the outfits that she wanted me and Ariel to wear. I just sat back and let her run around like a chicken with her head cut off. I went into the kitchen to get hors d'oeuvres. Then it hit me. If Brandy left, I'd be alone! I maintained myself as calmly as I could. After all, I wanted to make a good impression with the recruiter.

The recruiter came in the door, and me and Ariel positioned ourselves on the couch, placing hors d'oeuvres in the middle of the table. I crossed my legs as if I wanted to intimidate him. Deep down, I didn't want Brandy to go. Then I would really be alone—especially if she took Ariel with her! I mean, I had practically raised Ariel. She called me Mama and Brandy by her name. I was not about to let all that go. No sir, I would have to get me a lawyer, if that was the case. Brandy introduced the recruiter.

"Micah, this is Mr. Lucas, the Air Force recruiter," she said.

Mr. Lucas went to shake my hand, but I just stared at him like he'd stolen something from me, because all I heard was blah, blah, blah. The only thing I could see was that this Mr. Lucas was trying to take my family away. At one point, Brandy became embarrassed and moved the conversation outside on the porch. Of course, I grew very impatient and worked my way outside. Brandy looked at me with a disturbed look. I had no idea what was coming. I couldn't take it no more.

"What, what is it?" I asked.

Brandy let out a long sigh and looked at me. "I can't take Ariel with me. I would have to sign her over to your custody to go into the military."

Even though Brandy was a part-time parent and almost got Ariel taken away by child services, I knew she loved Ariel.

"Look, Brandy, this is your chance to do something. You know, like getting out of this old country town. Ariel will always be taken care of, and once you get settled, she can come and live with you again. Maybe we can both come and live with you, but you got to get through basic training."

Brandy looked relieved. I knew she wanted to get out of there and be somebody. It wasn't easy coming from a long line of drunks. Brandy hugged me tightly, like I was an angel saving her from hell. Then she whispered in my ear, "Thank you, my sister."

That was the closest I had ever felt to Brandy. From day one, Grandma Bean had seen something special in that girl, always inviting herself over and trying to be a part of our family. Grandma Bean intercepted her life in order to bring forth something good. What would have happened if she hadn't?

The recruiter interrupted. "Great. Everything is settled," Mr. Lucas said.

The recruiter tipped his hat and dusted off his clean and perfectly starched uniform before heading down the stairs. Oh, Lord, I couldn't believe it. Here came big trouble stumping up the driveway, practically knocking down the recruiter as he left the driveway. She was swinging her arms and switching her hips, with a stern look on her face.

It was Rochelle. She must have just got out of rehab, because she had filled out some in her face. Whenever she got out of rehab, she always came back a little heavier. Rochelle's social worker had put her in rehab again. They'd found a family to adopt the young kids, but the older kids kept acting up. No family wanted them. I heard that when they terminated her rights in court, she went a-cussing and fussing at the judge. They had to restrain her and escort the family out of the courtroom, because Rochelle had threatened to saw their heads off and stuff cucumbers up their butts!

I don't know how she would act if *all* her kids were adopted. Even though she'd lost custody of some of the kids, they were still hers. I think that's what bothered Rochelle the most; she had no control over herself or her children. I shuddered to think what was going to come out of her mouth next.

"Where my beans at, girl?" she shouted.

I couldn't believe this woman was confronting me over some beans. Brandy and I stood there for a moment with puzzled looks on our faces. "What are you talking about?" I asked.

Rochelle put her hands on her hips as if she was getting ready to read me, right there and right now! "You know what I'm talking about, gal! Your Grandma Bean made you give me beans for me and my children to eat forever. Why you all of a sudden stop giving me them beans? Social Service gonna try and take my kids if you stop giving me the damn beans." Rochelle looked as if she was truly confused.

Brandy leaned over and whispered to me. "Is she high?" she asked.

At the moment, I realized that she was not only high, but dirty and funky-smelling. Rochelle looked at us like something was wrong with us.

"Look, you need to give me my beans so I can feed my kids. Them magic beans, they keep us from starving!" she said.

Rochelle was delusional. I didn't know what she was talking about. Obviously, in her mind, she still had her children. I felt sorry for her, but Brandy didn't.

"Rochelle, listen to my voice. You ain't got no kids!" Brandy said.

Rochelle put her hand on her hip, turned around, and marched down the driveway yelling.

"You, heifers!" she shouted.

All you could see was dust kicking up from her heels.

Chapter Twenty-Five

It was the first time I could remember sitting in church by myself. Brandy had been gone for about a month. It was just me and Ariel. Shana came by when she was in town. Shana was a news reporter now in Atlanta, Georgia. Oh, how I envied her! She was living the good life in the big city!

Pastor Jacobs was preaching up something good this morning. I remembered how Grandma Bean would sit and say "Yes Lord!" to every word Pastor Jacobs said. I knew I wasn't where I needed to be spiritually. One day I'd rededicate myself to the Lord. Perhaps when I was married, I thought.

Pastor Jacobs wanted to talk with me after church was over and asked, "So Micah, how are things going?"

"Things are going well, Pastor Jacobs," I replied. "I just been having my hands full with Ariel and all."

Pastor Jacobs responded slowly, but I knew what he was getting at.

"Well, I haven't seen you since Ariel's christening," he said. "You know, God has a lot of things in store for you, Micah, if you'd just let him take the lead."

I couldn't really answer that; I was at a loss for words. Just then, I felt someone tapping me on the shoulder. I turned around to see Mr. McDaniel, Linwood's father, staring at me.

"Mr. McDaniel! I haven't seen you in a long time. How are you?" I asked.

"I'm doing good," he replied. "I got remarried and came back here. My wife's hometown is thirty minutes outside of town so this is closer."

I was happy for Mr. McDaniel. He really deserved someone nice. He was lonely after Linwood's mother died. I never thought he would move on and marry someone else.

"You know, Linwood is in the Air Force and is doing pretty good," he said. "You should give him a call. I know he would love to hear from you."

Before I could even say yes or no, Mr. McDaniel was handing me a piece of paper with Linwood's phone number. I couldn't believe I had his phone number right there in my hand. A nervous feeling came over me. What if he didn't want to see me again?

"Now you be sure, Micah, and call him tonight," he said.

"I will, Mr. McDaniel!" I said.

Mr. McDaniel gave me a big hug and left the room.

That night I kept pacing the floor, wondering if I should call or not. My stomach was in knots. I went back and forth in my mind—should I or shouldn't I? I was nervous and my hands were almost shaking. I wrestled with the thought of calling him. Before I knew it, my fingers were dialing his number. I was gonna hang up when someone answered. But I didn't.

Then a deep voice answered on the other end and said, "Hello?"

I couldn't breathe. I had thought about him over the years, but I couldn't believe I was actually talking to him.

"Hello? Can I speak to Linwood?" I asked.

"This is him. Who is this?"

"This is someone you haven't spoken to since high school," I said.

I heard him on the other end, trying to figure out who I was. I mean, I just could not believe I was talking to him. All of a sudden, I couldn't hold it in anymore.

"Linwood, it's me, Micah!" I said.

I heard him sigh on the other end of the phone. Then he said, "You are not going to believe me, but I was going to say it was you! Oh, my God, I haven't talked to you in so long. Let's see, the last thing I heard about you was that you had started beauty school."

"I did start beauty school. I only needed a couple more classes to finish. I started and stopped so many times that it was ridiculous. I'm kind of raising Brandy's child Ariel while she's stationed in Texas. Brandy's also in the Air Force, and I think she's gonna get out this year. Brandy missed Ariel terribly, but with all that running around, she couldn't keep her. And Shana works for the news station in Atlanta. Let's see, the last time I saw you, you got saved."

"I did, and I am still saved," he said proudly.

"Well, where are you?" I asked. "What city did I call? What do you do in the Air Force?"

I'm actually in Atlanta, Georgia," he said. "My dad is moving closer your way, though. I will be in town real soon. We should get together."

"That would be great," I replied.

I could feel him smiling through the phone. I wondered if he could feel me smiling as well. I paused.

"Hey, are you married?" he asked. "Do you have any kids of your own?"

"No, I'm not married, and, no, I don't have kids of my own. What about you?" I asked. To tell the truth, I was afraid of his answer. What if he was married? Then I'd look like a fool.

"No, I'm not married, and no kids here either," he said. "I would love to be married, though. Well, I have to go. I guess I'll see you soon."

"Okay, see you soon."

I never felt so much relief in my life! The whole night, I tossed and turned. Part of me had thought I would never see him again. I wondered if he was still as handsome as he was before? Ariel was lying down and woke from her sleep. She looked at me as if she was definitely puzzled by my happiness. I had basically put my whole personal life on hold to raise Ariel. Brandy would come and see her, and believe you me, she knew who her mother was. Soon as I thought I was getting comfortable, the phone rang. It was Brandy.

"Hey, girl, what up? It's Brandy," she said.

"Hey, how you doing?" I replied.

"Fine," she said. "How's Ariel? I miss my baby so much. Well, I was actually calling you because I will be out of the Air Force at the end of the month, which means Ariel can come and live with me."

My heart fell. Don't get me wrong—Ariel has a relationship with her mother. Brandy comes to visit all the time. But I really had not planned on her returning home so soon. I mean, I know that a mother is supposed to be with her child, but that would leave me all alone. What would I do all by myself?

"Brandy, do you think now is a good time for Ariel to get adjusted to a new home? I'm not sure it's a good time to take her back."

"Now is the best time, before school starts," she said. "I mean, I don't want her starting school there and then have to transfer her down here."

"But Brandy, she's only three years old," I said.

"I know that, but I miss her, and besides, she's my child. I mean I had her."

I couldn't argue with that. Ariel was her child, and I knew it would be best for Ariel.

"Well, when are you coming down to get her?" I asked.

"I was thinking I would come the first of the month."

"You got a job lined up?" I asked.

"Of course. I didn't stay in the military for nothing. I got an associate's degree in computers. They hired me at this computer company."

Things grew quiet on the phone. Brandy knew this was as difficult for me as for her.

"Micah, it's not like you will never see her again," she said. "You know, we'll always come back home there. But it's time for her to come live with me. I'll be settled in my apartment by the end of the month. I'll come down to get her then."

Before I could say anything on the phone, Brandy was saying she loved me and she would talk to me later. Then she hung up the phone. I looked at Ariel. I couldn't believe she was leaving me. Now, with Ariel going to live with Brandy, I would be all alone.

The next morning, I was awfully tired. Ariel had kept me up most of the night, tossing and turning, but she was my "Booky," whether she annoyed me or not. Just as I was about to fix breakfast, the phone rang.

"Hello."

"Hey, girl, it's me, Shana."

"Oh, what's going on?" I asked.

"I'm in town for the weekend," she said. "What's going on? You gotta work?"

"No," I replied. "Actually, I'm off today."

"Well, let's meet up for breakfast and hang out today," she said.

That sounded like a good idea. I mean, I really didn't feel like cooking while still being tired and all.

"Okay. What time you wanna meet?" I asked.

"How about thirty minutes?" she asked. "We can go to the waffle house."

"That's cool," I said. "Come by and scoop me in thirty minutes."

"All right, Micah. See you in thirty minutes, and be ready!"

"I will!"

I hurried to dress. After all, I wanted to eat. I was hungry!

Breakfast was good. As I was biting into my country ham, Shana dropped her fork and folded her arms while giving me that "you holding back on me" look.

"What?" I asked. "Why are you staring at me like that?"

"As if you don't know already," she said. "Did you get a call from Linwood?"

I mean, I could not believe she knew about that phone call. I knew Shana had all the inside scoop, but I didn't realize she had *my* inside scoop!

"Who did you hear that from? Better yet, *how* did you hear that? I don't remember telling you?"

"Now, you know I can't reveal my sources! All I need to know is if it's true." Shana looked at me as if she demanded an answer, as if she had a right to know.

"If you must know, yes, I talked to him."

I intentionally left it like that so she wouldn't intrude in my life, but that didn't make any difference. I mean, she didn't become a news reporter for nothing. She was gonna get the final story if it killed her.

"So, Micah, you mean to tell me that you didn't feel anything when you talked to Linwood?" she asked. "Really, Micah . . . as much as you were in love with him?"

"I'm not gonna sit here and lie," I said. "It was good talking to him again."

Shana looked at me as if she was waiting for more. "And?" she said.

"And I haven't heard from him since then," I replied. "So I'm not trying to really think about it, ya know?"

"Okay," she said, "you get back in touch with the love of your life, and you mean to tell me that you're not thinking about him or nothing? I don't believe that!"

"I'm just saying we're in two different spaces. He's saved . . . I'm not. He has everything going for him. I have so many issues—I mean, how could that possibly work?"

"I'm not saying that you all just jump into something. But! Don't just cut him off like that," she said. Shana always saw the possible in the impossible. Personally, I didn't see it working."

"I hear you," I said, "but the bottom line is, I haven't heard from him, so case closed!"

Shana began to eat her breakfast again, as if she hadn't heard me. Then she changed the subject.

"So, when's Brandy coming to get Ariel?" she asked.

"In three more weeks, supposedly," I replied.

Shana dropped her fork again.

"So, then, what you gonna do after Ariel's gone?" she asked. "Maybe you should think about selling the house and moving in with me."

"I thought about that, but I'm almost finished with school, and I wouldn't want to jeopardize that," I said.

"You mean you're scared!"

I hated to admit it, but I *was* scared. What else would I do with my life?

Chapter Twenty-Six

Saturdays were pretty busy at Carmen's hair salon. By 10:00 a.m. I had washed so many heads, it was pathetic. And that was the day that everybody either wanted a perm or hair weave. I knew that I was capable of running the shop myself. Half the time, Carmen was out running errands while I was taking care of things anyway. I was washing this young lady's hair, and it was kinky. I mean, it felt like my fingers were being cut up. I put some conditioner on her hair and got her under the dryer.

Then, here *she* come, walking in like she got an attitude: Rochelle. And surprisingly, her social worker was right behind her. Rochelle sat down in my chair. Boy did she stink! Looked like she had been on an all-night binge. She was high as a kite! Rochelle looked at me like I was moving too slow.

"Now, make me beautiful!" Rochelle said.

I paused for a second and thought about it. I knew that nothing I could do would make this child beautiful.

Ms. Williams gave me a look as if she really wanted me to do Rochelle's hair. She came over to me and pulled me to the side and said, "Um, she has an interview for in-patient drug treatment. We got someone to sponsor her makeover, so the bill will be paid for."

I looked at Rochelle. She stuck out her tongue at me. Then I turned my attention back to Ms. Williams. "I didn't know social services had a program that paid for people's hair to be done?" I said.

Rochelle rudely interrupted. "My social worker cares about *me*!" she yelled. "She the only one out of all y'all that gives a damn about me! At least I'm trying to get clean!"

I had to admit that for once I would like to know what Rochelle looked like drug-free.

"Okay, Ms. Rochelle," I said. "I'll do my best to make you beautiful."

Ms. Williams let out a big sigh of relief and sat down. Poor Ms. Williams. She must really love her job, because she was working harder than Rochelle to get her kids out of foster care. Ms. Williams was an educated, well-spoken, young white woman. Rochelle's case was the first she'd ever had at social services. Rochelle had been reported to child welfare so many times, everyone knew her down there, and the old social workers didn't want her case.

I put a cape around Rochelle's neck and proceeded to check her scalp.

"Well, well, well," I said. "Looks like you will have to reschedule with Carmen."

Rochelle looked at me with a puzzled expression on her face. "Why can't you do my hair?" she asked.

"Well, I don't mind doing your hair, Rochelle, but there's one problem."

"What's that?" she asked.

"You've got head lice!"

Working at the shop all day was exhausting. Luckily for me, Ariel was staying the night with Shana. I felt nasty after looking at the lice on Rochelle's head. She wouldn't be going to the treatment center right away. So there I was, soaking in the bathtub, getting the nasty out of me.

I hadn't had time to really be on the dating scene. Of course, I'd never been one to date around. I mean, I really didn't want to be anything like my mother. I closed my eyes and relaxed. Lately, I'd realized that my life was so routine. I had been feeling as if I really wanted someone in my life.

At that point, there were mostly women in my life who had loved me. Cherish, Grandma Bean, Shana, and of course Brandy. I hadn't really, truly been in love. But now at the age of twenty-five, I wanted to be loved.

Shana and Brandy were both moving on with their lives. Brandy had someone special, and Shana was a man-magnet! I just wanted someone special in my life too. *Dear Lord, if you're listening, please send me someone to love me for me.* When I opened my eyes, the phone rang.

"Hello?" I said.

"Hello, can I speak to Micah?"

"This is she," I said.

"This is Linwood. How are you?"

I could not believe he'd called back! I had not been expecting this at all. "I'm good," I said. "I can't complain."

"Well, you were on my mind," he said. "I thought I would give you a call. It's been a long time since we seen each other. What do you look like?"

Now, I thought that was just vain! The first thing he wanted to know was what I looked like?

"I'm big, fat, and ugly!" I said.

Linwood laughed. "Come on now! I was expecting some women to be fat, but you didn't gain that much weight, did you?"

"No," I said. "I gained about fifteen pounds since the last time I saw you."

"That's not bad at all," he said. "I gained some weight also."

Now, that I couldn't believe. Linwood was always a very thin guy. "Well, you could stand to gain a little weight," I said.

I could tell that Linwood was dancing around me, trying to figure me out.

"So you know, I'll be in town tomorrow. Maybe I can stop by. I mean, ya know, I want to see you."

As much as I wanted to see Linwood, I was also nervous about it. What if he didn't like what he saw? "Um, I got a hair appointment on tomorrow," I said.

"You won't be in the salon all day. When you get out, give me a call, and I'll stop by."

"Okay, I'll call you tomorrow," I said. "I might have Ariel with me."

"Well, I'll see you tomorrow and sweet dreams," he said.

"Sweet dreams to you Linwood."

I was nervous all day. I had on my best pantsuit outfit. I had just come from Carmen's because I had to get my hair done. As I drove up to my house, Linwood was waiting outside, standing beside a Cadillac. My heart was beating so fast. Linwood was much taller and thinner. Not much had changed physically since the last time I saw him. I slowly got out of the car. I really didn't know what he would think of me. Immediately, he came up and hugged me.

"Hey, girl, you look great!" he said. He immediately grabbed my hand and held it for a while.

"You still have Grandma Bean's house," he said. "That's good." He looked at the house and then said, "Not much has changed." He gave me a big smile. He always did have a nice smile. I was anxious to know what he had been up to.

"Well, come on in," I said. "We got a lot of catching up to do."

Linwood followed me into the house and made himself comfortable on the living room chair. I could tell he was waiting for me to strike up a conversation.

"So, what is it that you do for a living?" I asked.

"I'm into real estate. I own a couple of properties in Atlanta. I buy them, then fix them up and sell them for a lot more. So basically, I'm into flipping property. I went to real estate school but decided to make my money work for me. So what career choice did you make?" he asked.

Okay, now how was I going to tell this man that I was a shampoo girl who had been trying to finish cosmetology school? I relaxed in my chair and then crossed my legs.

"Well, the most important thing I have done is to take care of Ariel. You know that takes a lot of time. Actually, Brandy will come and pick her up tomorrow to live with her in Texas. I'm in cosmetology school, and I do hair at Carmen's now. You remember Carmen, right?" I asked.

"Yeah, it's good she still has her business going and stuff. So what about you and your mom?" he asked. "Is her situation still the same?"

Linwood was putting it very lightly. Mom had been locked up for a long time now.

"Well, she's still locked up," I replied.

Linwood leaned in toward me and asked, "Have you forgiven her?"

This angered me. I knew what he was talking about. He was talking about Cherish's death. "I haven't forgotten what she did," I said. "I barely see her. I don't make an effort to see her."

Linwood leaned back in the chair and let out a big sigh.

"So you haven't forgiven her," he said. Linwood gave me that *aha* look.

"Look, Linwood," I said. "Your mom isn't the one sitting in a jail cell for a murder she didn't commit. Your mom didn't take the rap for some man who's out on the street, roaming free." At that point, I was getting upset, and Linwood knew it. He grabbed my hand and caressed it while attempting to comfort me.

"You can't be free unless you learn to forgive," he said.

"How do I do that, Linwood?" I asked.

"By accepting Jesus Christ as your Lord and personal savior," he replied.

I thought about that. It was a big commitment for me. I mean, you have to be perfect and flawless to be saved. I would definitely be living under a microscope. I always thought I would get saved when I was married. I always thought I would have dealt with my demons by then.

"I'm sorry, Linwood," I said. "I'm not ready to do that. After all, you can fool a lot of people, but you can't fool Jesus!"

Chapter Twenty-Seven

I slept hard that night. I tossed and turned in the bed, thinking about the things Linwood had said to me. When I woke up the next morning, my back was very stiff and sore. I had convinced myself that Linwood didn't know what he was talking about. Brandy was on her way to pick up Ariel this morning anyway. I was scurrying to pack the rest of her bags and get dressed. The phone rang. I hoped it was Brandy, because I really wasn't ready yet.

"Hello."

"Collect call from Central Prison. Will you accept the charges?"

I hesitated for a moment. I knew it was Irish. Then she yelled through the phone operator for me to accept the charges.

"Yes, I'll accept charges," I said.

"Hey, girl, it's your mom, Irish."

I couldn't say I was happy to hear from her.

"Well, I was wondering when you were going to come see your mom," she said. "It's been a long time since I seen you.

Grandma Bean wouldn't like it if you didn't come see me for my birthday!"

My mother knew that even after death I still respected my grandmother's wishes.

"Well, are you coming?" she asked.

"Yeah, I'm coming," I replied. "Brandy will be here to pick up Ariel, and then I'll be by there. I can't promise I'll stay long, though. I have a lot of other things to do. Plus, I need to put some fresh flowers on Grandma Bean's grave."

Mama hesitated when answering back. I could tell she wasn't happy with what I said, but I honestly did have things to do. And besides, she wasn't going nowhere, being in prison.

"There you go again, putting ya Grandma Bean before your own mama," she said. "All I'm asking for you to do is come visit me. Is that too much ask?"

You know, I really didn't feel like getting into an argument with my mother at that moment.

"Irish, I will see you in a little bit," I said.

I didn't even give Mama a chance to finish the conversation. I kindly hung up the phone.

By the time Brandy arrived, Ariel had fallen asleep again. And Brandy didn't come alone. She came strolling up with a nerdy-looking guy. She introduced him as her boyfriend Dexter. Now, I could not see these two as a couple, but according to Brandy, they were.

"Micah, you really look good, and I missed you so much! Where's Ariel?" she asked. She came over to hug me. I had missed her too. Actually, Brandy looked as though she'd lost some weight.

"You look good too," I said. "Ariel is upstairs, asleep. So how did you and Dexter meet?"

Dexter anxiously answered the question. He seemed to want to cater to Brandy.
"We met at work," he said. "We both were into computer programming. Brandy likes computers as much as I do. I started my business where we go and fix computers—for a small fee of course."

I could tell that Dexter was nervous. He probably wanted to make a good impression or something like that.

"Of course," I said. "I mean, you all have to make a living."

Dexter seemed to go into a relaxed mode after I said that. He leaned back in the chair and uncrossed his legs. Then he blurted out something that none of us was expecting.

"Yeah, especially when you got a little one on the way!" he said.

Brandy swatted Dexter on the arm. Oh, so they were gonna keep this a secret? I jumped up and grabbed Brandy by the arm. "In the kitchen—now!" I shouted at Brandy.

I flung open the kitchen door and forced Brandy to sit down at the table. A million thoughts were going through my head. I mean, what was she thinking? *Was* she thinking? Another baby on the way, and you just getting your daughter back? I paced the floor up and down, huffing and puffing. Brandy looked like a deer caught in the headlights. Then she had the nerve to blurt out: "Look, I'm a grown woman!"

That comment in itself stopped me in my tracks. I threw my hands in the air as if to say, *I give up.*

"Brandy, you just got Ariel back!" I said.

"You talking like she was in foster care or something," she said. "I mean, I let you keep her while I was getting stationed all over the world. I did something with my life! You the one who put their life on pause after Cherish died!" Brandy stopped in her tracks after realizing what she'd said. Then she stepped toward me and tried to console me.

"Oh God, Micah, I'm sorry! I didn't mean to . . . I didn't mean . . ."

I raised my hand up, signaling Brandy to be quiet. Feelings of anger and hurt welled up inside me. "You know what, Brandy? I think it's time for you to go," I said.

I left it at that and went upstairs to my bedroom. Five minutes later, I watched as Brandy, Dexter, and Ariel left the house. All I could see was Brandy looking back at the window where I stood. Brandy was right. After Cherish died, it was as if my life just stopped. I had been taking cosmetology classes forever. By then, I should have been finished. I felt needed when I was taking care of Ariel. I didn't know if Ariel's leaving was a blessing or a curse. I definitely needed answers for myself.

I hated going to the prison to see Mama. A feeling of heaviness always came over me. The feeling was heavier this morning. I was still dealing with everything that happened between Brandy and me. My mind was in another place. I really don't even remember being searched by the guard. Mama came strolling in with a smile on her face. Then she stopped and started singing. "Happy birthday to me!" she shouted.

"Happy birthday, Mama," I said.

I mean, really, who celebrates their birthday in prison? Mama had lost weight. The first years of prison had been rough on her. After all, prison was no safe place for accused child murderers, and the fact that Cherish had been raped didn't make it any easier. Mama got into fights for being plain stupid! Most people figured Woody had killed Cherish. Even the district attorney became frustrated, because he really wanted Woody in prison. He had been trying to catch Woody for a long time, and he knew Mama held the key to some valuable information concerning a lot of Woody's crimes. Of course, Mama never gave in. Her loyalty to Woody was more important than the truth.

So there I was, visiting someone who had chosen to be a convict rather than a mother to me. Mama had tried and convicted my love a long time ago, and I wasn't sure I would ever be free to love her, not like she wanted me to.

"Hello, Micah," she said. "I don't get that much time for visiting, ya know." Mama was trying to get my attention.

"Yes, ma'am, I know," I replied.

"So, how's things going?" she asked.

"Things are going okay. It's just been kind of hard with Grandma Bean not here. I've been really going through some things." Mama seemed to become a little bit annoyed, and I didn't understand why. "Okay, what is it?" I asked.

"Ya know, for once I thought you came here to visit me," she said. "At least you can talk to me about the things going on with you. Ya Grandma Bean ain't here no more! So ya gonna have to start dealing with me, ya real mama. The one who *chose* to have you!"

I couldn't believe she was acting like this. Why would I feel comfortable talking to her? I only had one mother. "Grandma Bean *was* my mother," I said.

Mama's face turned stone cold. Then she leaned toward me and said, "You think ya Grandma Bean was such an angel? Well, why don't you ask your God to show you the truth? My mama was just like me! Where do you think I got it from? There's a long line of trifling women in our family. It's in your blood. You think what I did to you was so bad? You don't know your precious Grandma Bean. She was just as messed up as me."

"You got some nerve talking about Grandma Bean!" I said. "You know what? This conversation is over. I'm leaving!"

I got up to leave. Mama got up and pushed her chair out of the way.

"Yeah, well, leave then! Asa Lama Lakum, sister!" she said.

As I walked from the visiting room, I turned back to my mama. I knew this was the last time I would see her for a long time.

"Good-bye, Mother."

Chapter Twenty-Eight

That night I had a dream that Mama was possessed by a demon. Me, Grandma Bean, and Brandy would make the devil flee, but he kept coming back to Mama. Then I was confused. How could the demon keep coming back? Then I realized that she allowed him to do so. They say, at all times good or evil dwells in you, but never at the same time. Where there's good, evil cannot be; where's there's evil, good cannot be.

I thought about people I knew who chose to let evil dwell in their bodies because they saw no room for good. *Dear Lord, please do not let evil consume me just because I'm related to it. God, please intercede and show me the truth.*

The choir was singing. It actually felt as though the church walls were shaking, as if God himself had touched the house. I looked out the windows, looked at the congregation. There I stood in front of Pastor Jacobs, while he smiled graciously at me. I had known that when this day came, he would be overjoyed. It was the day of my birth and death. I had received Christ that morning, and through Christ there was life. The old me was dead.

I felt the burdens lift off me, just as though dead skin was being sloughed off. Yes, this was a new beginning. After Pastor Jacobs prayed over me, he looked at the congregation. He appeared to be searching for someone. He started to walk up and down the aisles as if he was searching for someone.

Most of the congregation was puzzled by this. Then he stopped when he reached the church doors. Pastor Jacobs turned to address the congregation.

"Where is Sister Rochelle?" he asked.

I didn't realize that Rochelle hadn't been in church for a while. Nobody noticed when a crackhead stopped coming to church, but Pastor Jacobs did. He looked for her throughout the congregation. Now, our church was located in the drug part of town, and right down the street was a crack house that operated 24/7, even on Sundays. I had a keen feeling Rochelle was there.

Pastor Jacobs had tried to run those drug dealers away, but they wouldn't go nowhere. This time, I could tell that Pastor Jacobs had had enough. He flung open the church doors. The congregation really didn't know what to do. Pastor Jacobs stepped outside, his black leather shoes hitting the ground. The dust traveled up his pants leg. Then, with every step, Pastor Jacobs started walking toward that old crack house, shouting all the way.

"The devil ain't gonna take our sister!" he yelled in a thunderous voice, and the congregation was right behind him.

Pastor Jacobs marched with steady force and authority. The congregation was steady behind Pastor Jacobs, marching with him. All I could think about was, *I declare war on the devil.* I had my head up high and marched along with the congregation, for on this day I'd given my life to Christ and joined the army of God. Why, then, should I let the devil take my sister?

We walked up to that old house with Pastor leading the way. He marched up the steps to that house and with one thrust tore down the screen door. Everybody in the house was startled. Drugs were everywhere. Some people were so high, they were stumbling all over the place. Then, there she was . . . Rochelle. She was so high, her lips suffered blisters and burns. Rochelle was clearly embarrassed and high, all at the same time. I looked for life in Rochelle's eyes, and all I saw was death.

Rochelle had the most beautiful sea-green eyes. Her skin was golden and looked as if it had been kissed by the sun. In my mind, I thought about the what-if's. What if Rochelle had chosen a natural high instead of a manmade one? What if she was high on life? What if on the day Rochelle was introduced to drugs, she'd said no instead of yes? What if she had refused to date a thug and had abstained from sex until marriage? What if she'd chosen God as a first choice rather than her last option? Only God knew the answers to my what if's. For now, I could only pray for what Rochelle *could* be. Pastor Jacobs began shouting angrily.

"Devil, you can't have our sister!" he shouted.

Pastor Jacobs scooped up Rochelle and passed her up and over people. Rochelle's lifeless body was lifted out of darkness and out of the crack house. The light pierced Rochelle's eyes. She squinted her eyes like a newborn baby looking at the world for the first time. I, of course, didn't know what to expect. I only knew that Rochelle and I finally had something in common. I knew that both our lives had been intercepted by God, and we would never be the same.

It was Mother's Day, and absolutely no one had called me to wish me a happy one. Then the phone rang. It was Linwood!

My heart sank to my stomach. Every time I talked with him, there was a feeling of surprise that rose up in me.

"Hey, Micah," he said. "I was just calling to say Happy Mother's Day."

"Happy Mother's Day? I'm not a mother!" I said.

Linwood laughed.

"But you will be one day," he said. "I was just gettin' a head start on it. Plus, have you forgot that you raised a little girl for the first three years of her life?"

"Ya know what? That's true. I didn't think about it like that. So how's your life?" I asked. Really, I just wanted to know if he'd gotten married or something. You see, Linwood was the only guy that I had pure innocent love for. If he was to get married, I didn't think I would even want to know about it.

"My life is good," he said. "My job is going well, so I can't complain. God is good all the time. I don't know where I would be without God. So how's your life?"

Linwood sounded happy. Normally, everyone I met didn't like their lives or their jobs. So this was definitely something different.

"My life is okay," I said, "but it's getting better." There were some hard things in my life, like my relationship with Mama and the fact that I was twenty-six years old with no career."

Linwood paused before responding. "I'll be in town tomorrow; we can discuss this over dinner," he said.

I didn't know what to say except *okay.*

"Okay."

Chapter Twenty-Nine

All day I went shopping, trying desperately to find the right outfit. I was no longer a size six. I remembered being able to eat anything and not gain a pound. The doorbell rang. I looked at my watch and noticed that Linwood was early. I threw on my dress, slipped on my shoes, and touched my hair. I fled down the stairs and opened the door. Linwood looked as handsome as ever. He looked like a gentleman. I mean, he even brung flowers.

"Hey, beautiful, you ready to go?" he asked.

I couldn't remember the last time anyone had called me beautiful. Actually, I was beginning to think that only white men said that. The whole way to the restaurant, I was rather quiet. Linwood would make small conversation. By the time we arrived at the restaurant, we were all small-talked out. Linwood wasted no time ordering his food. He appeared very professional and cordial to our waitress. I could tell he was used to going to fancy places. It was almost a little bit intimidating. Linwood looked at me as if he was concerned.

"You all right?" he asked.

I tried to play it off.

"What were you thinking about, your mom?" he asked.

Now, why on earth would Linwood ask me that? He knew what my mom had done and where she was at. "Why on earth would I be thinking about that woman?" I asked.

Linwood gave me a surprised look.

"Because she is still your mother, and the Bible do tell you to honor thy mother and thy father," he said. "Remember?"

"Well, God definitely wasn't talking about her," I said.

Linwood looked at me as if I had just cursed him out or something. "Look, Micah. What your mother did and who she took the rap for . . . well, right now it's all about you becoming healthy through God's word. The only way to do that is through forgiveness. It may not make since, but you have to forgive her—for yourself. If you don't learn to forgive her, then it will eat you up on the inside like a cancer."

"You don't know how I feel," I said. "Your mother isn't supposed to turn her back on you or choose a man over the truth. Sometimes at night I wake up so angry at her that I pound my fist into the mattress pretending it's her face. I'm so mad at her because she doesn't hold the same family values. I can't believe I even came out of her. She's the spawn of Satan!" I yelled.

Linwood gently wiped his mouth, took a sip of water, and replied, "The devil will always try and go through your family if he can. Remember what happened to Joseph in the Bible? His own brothers did him wrong and turned their backs on him, but in the end their plan to destroy him failed, and God's plan to bless him succeeded. And remember, in the end, Joseph forgave them."

What had started as an evening I'd anticipated ended as a day I couldn't wait to be over. The drive home was quiet. I think Linwood felt that I was upset with him. I wasn't really upset with him, just upset with the whole situation. Did being a Christian mean I had to forgive people I didn't feel deserved to be forgiven? Family was supposed to stick together. The thing that made me sick to my stomach was that I couldn't understand how could she betray me. Wasn't there a part in her body that said, my child comes before any man?

As we drove up to the house, I sat there looking at Linwood, wondering how he did it. He came to an abrupt stop. He walked over and opened the door for me, took my hand, and walked me to the door. I didn't think he wanted to talk to me anymore that night, so I tried to make it short with him.

"Well, I guess this is good-night," I said.

Linwood look surprised. "Look, Micah," he said. "You may not see what I'm saying right now, but hopefully one day you will. I really don't want to talk anymore about your mother."

I felt an immediate sigh of relief. "I don't want to talk about this anymore myself," I said.

Linwood leaned over and kissed my forehead. "I'll call you tomorrow," he said.

I walked inside the house and peeked out the window to see Linwood driving off into the night. I thought to myself, *Yeah, right. I'll never hear from him again. He probably thinks I'm too much maintenance and come with too much baggage. On that note, I think I'll turn into bed.*

The phone rang early the next morning. For a minute, I thought it might be Carmen calling, trying to get me to come in early. I checked the caller ID and it was Brandy.

"Hey, Brandy."

185

"Hey, Micah, I was just calling to see how you were doing and stuff."

Brandy, of all people, knew I was definitely not a morning person. I looked at the clock to check the time.

"I mean, ya know, it's 6:30 in the morning," I said. I could tell something was wrong. Brandy was becoming increasingly agitated.

"What's wrong, Brandy?" I asked.

"Why does something have to be wrong every time I call you?" she asked.

Now Brandy and I both knew that she was beating around the bush. I figured if that was the game she wanted to play, then we could play that game. I started to act like nothing was wrong, like I wasn't really interested in what she had to say. Brandy grew just a little bit frustrated on the other end of the phone. She could tell I was on to her.

"Okay, okay, Micah! I need to tell you that . . . well, you already know I'm pregnant."

Yeah, I already knew she was pregnant again because Dexter couldn't keep a secret. Brandy had been a wonder ever since I'd known her. Biologically, she was an only child. Her mom didn't have any other kids. Now, I knew Grandma Bean didn't know too much about Brandy's parents, besides the fact that their names were Peggy and Xavier Dunn. If you let Brandy tell it, her mom didn't want any other children. I suspected that Brandy had gotten pregnant on purpose. Family always meant stability to Brandy.

"Well, how far along are you?" I asked.

"Two months," she replied.

"How does Dexter feel about the baby?" I asked.

Brandy took a long pause. I was very unsure about her answer. "He doesn't want the baby," she said. "So I'm moving out. Actually, that has something to do with why I'm calling. I didn't re-enlist in the Air Force and Dexter and I split up, so I was wondering if I could move back home. I don't need you to lecture me right now. I just need your support."

"Brandy, you know you can come home whenever you are ready," I said. "Besides, I was getting really lonely by myself. I was about to start exercising, anyway. I could lose some of this fat. Girl, you would not believe that I am up to 137 pounds!"

"What? You, Micah?" she said. "Now you know you have definitely always been a skinny-minny! Just like Grandma Bean, only with a little butt!"

We both fell out laughing. The truth was, I loved Brandy and Ariel. They were definitely my family, and family stuck together.

"Do you remember when you thought the size of your butt was the only thing keeping Linwood?" she asked. She laughed out loud. "Hah! That little booty?"

"I don't know what was I thinking?" I replied.

"Hey, did Linwood ever call you back? Did you hear anything else from him?"

"Actually, he came to see me yesterday," I said. "We had a date."

"What? And you ain't tell nobody?" she asked. "I need to know every detail. Did y'all kiss or anything?"

"He was a perfect gentleman," she said, "and because it's early, I will definitely tell you the rest later!" I yawned. I really was tired. I could tell Brandy was disappointed, but she was yawning herself.

"Okay," she said, "but don't leave out any details, and call me first thing in the morning. And Micah, I love you."

"I love you too, Brandy. Give Ariel a kiss good-night for me."

"Okay," she said.

"Good-night."

I must have been real tired. Granted, I had stayed up late the night before, way past my bedtime. Have you ever been awake on the inside, but your body was asleep on the outside and you couldn't wake up? Well, that was what I was experiencing. I began to see visions of me in a courtroom, and the judge was telling me that I had been convicted. I kept trying talk to my lawyer and ask what was I convicted of. The next vision I had, I was being led to a jail cell, and then the iron doors slammed shut. I couldn't get out, and it didn't matter how hard I screamed. My anger had consumed me. I had become a very destructive woman and, worse, Linwood and I never met up again. The vision scared me, and I prayed to God to help me. I repeated it over and over again. *Help me, Lord.*

My lips began to move, and feeling came back to my body. I continued to ask God to help me. I woke up in a panic-sweat. Fear flushed through my body. I was also quite sweaty from tossing and turning through the night. It seemed as if I'd closed my eyes for only a moment, but it was actually morning when I woke up. I knew then that God had to be number one in my life. I was actually afraid to imagine myself without God.

There was no turning back, only moving forward. I know what I had to do in order to be set free. Linwood was right. I had to learn to forgive Mama. Hating her would only eat me up like a cancer, and at that point, I refused to give her that power. I had to let my love out of jail and set it free. My love would no longer be held captive by my anger toward Mama. I laid my head back down on the pillow. Tomorrow, I thought, I knew what I needed to do.

Chapter Thirty

I got dressed early in the morning, and I actually looked like a young lady. Linwood had left me a telephone message. I must have been asleep hard; I didn't remember the phone ever ringing. He wanted to let me know that he was going to stop by that evening. I grabbed my purse and keys and headed for the car. As I was traveling down the highway, I thought about everything that had happened to lead me to that point. And suddenly I began to thank and praise God for deliverance. I felt relieved to know I didn't have to worry about my life anymore. I thought about Linwood and how free he was.

I know it may sound crazy, but we could never be together unless I became free too. I found myself having feelings; I knew I cared for him. The feelings were as fresh as the day I'd met him. It was like time had never passed. There was a bond between us so strong that time could not break it. I felt a rush of anger come to me. I was angry that I had waited so long to do this. I was angry about all the time I'd wasted being mad, sad, or angry when I could have been enjoying happiness. But then, I thought, maybe Linwood had to go away to grow in God. Maybe Brandy had to move; maybe Ariel had to leave and go back to Brandy for God to get me alone with him. God doesn't care about time, but timing is everything to him. As I pulled into the prison gates, I thought to myself, *Yeah, God doesn't recognize time. Look how long Mama's been in prison. Ten years she's been in prison for something she didn't do.*

I couldn't understand why someone would take the fall for something they didn't do. I would think, since Grandma Bean had died, that she would want to be with me. I would think that when Cherish died, she would have wanted to be there for me, but she hadn't wanted to be with me at all. Mama had made her choice, and it involved sacrificing herself for Woody before being a mom to me. In order for me to move on and be released from anger, I had to forgive her.

I don't know how I made it through security. Lord knows, I was so nervous that morning, I forgot to take out all my metal. Before I knew it, they were bringing Mama in to see me. Mama smiled as if she was happy to see me. I smiled back, and for once it wasn't a fake smile but a real one. I knew that, no matter what, there would be a resolution today between myself and her. *God, please give me the strength to confront Mama and forgive her. I don't know how you'll do it, but I am willing to be a vessel for you to use me today.* Mama pointed for me to pick up the phone.

"Hey, baby girl. I'm glad you finely got a chance to visit me. How's everybody doing?" she asked.

I looked at her with a puzzled look. Now, she knew we ain't the best of friends, so I don't even know why she was trying to act like that.

"I come to see you so that maybe I can get some answers to my questions," I said.

Mama looked puzzled now. "All right," she said. "What do you need to know?"

"Why did you take the fall for killing Cherish? Why didn't you let Woody go to prison for it like he should have?"

Mama took a long, deep breath and replied, "Well, what happened, happened. It's been a long time now. Let it go."

I couldn't believe she was so casual about shutting down this subject.

"Let it go? Let it go? My best friend was raped and murdered by your white boyfriend!"

Mama slammed her hand down with anger. "That white boyfriend is getting ready to be my husband!" she said.

"Husband?" I said. "Mama, he barely comes to visit you! He got you in a jail cell, while he's out selling drugs. How could you cover up for him and take the rap?"

Mama started crying hysterically. "This is a majority black town!" she cried. "If he had pleaded guilty, they would have killed him for sure, and I couldn't live with that!"

I stood up and prepared myself to leave. There was really nothing else to say.

"Well, Mama, you couldn't live with the fact that he could have been sentenced to death, but you can live with the fact that he killed my best friend? You make me live with that every day. Don't worry; I forgive you. I have to in order to be released from you. Yes, Mama, I forgive you. I win!" I began to walk away.

"Micah—Asa Lama Lakum, sister!" she shouted.

I turned to look at Mama. "May God have mercy on your soul, Mama," I replied.

The drive home consisted of me and silence. What could be said after what had just happened? Half an hour later, I was pulling up to the house, only to see Brandy and Ariel sitting on the porch. Actually, I'd never been so happy to see them. Ariel came up and hugged me. God, she was a breath of fresh air. Ariel was the picture of innocence. She loved me, but more importantly, she loved her mother. Children are so forgiving. No matter what Brandy had done to her, Ariel still loved her. Brandy stood on the porch with open arms. I went to hug her. Brandy held me tight, then pulled back to look at me.

"You know you gonna be stuck with me for a while, right?" she said.

After being alone for a while, I had come to appreciate company, and Brandy and Ariel were more than company. God had placed them in my life as the sister I'd never had and niece I'd always wanted. I gave Brandy the biggest smile.

"This is your home too. You have just as much right to stay here as me. Grandma Bean was your grandma too. Now, how would she feel if her grandchildren had no place to stay?"

Brandy gave me a slight smile. I remembered back to when I'd met Brandy and how I'd tried to leave her out of my life. Grandma Bean had seen something extraordinary about her. Grandma Bean had known she would be the sister I would need. Grandma Bean used to say one of her favorite scriptures: "It is not good for man to be alone."

Brandy draped her arm around my shoulder. I grabbed Ariel's hand, and we all walked toward the front door. Brandy stopped abruptly in her tracks.

"Oh, and by the way, Linwood called," she said. "He left a message for you, letting you know he would come by around 9:00 a.m., and maybe y'all could have breakfast or something. He said he was stuck at the office and would leave early in the morning."

This morning when I woke up, I'd felt different. I felt as though there were definitely some things I wanted to change in my life. I was going to take charge of my life. I had decided to start with changing my weight. I figured I could get a quick workout in before Linwood came by. I put my Walkman on the country music station and began to run through the neighborhood. My thighs jiggled as I ran to the rhythm of the country music. I was in a zone, and all of a sudden I felt strong. I had faced my past and was moving forward in my life. Sweat beads began to form on my face, but the wind blew the sweat away. It felt as if God was saying, "Don't worry. Just leave the past behind you."

One mile turned into two miles and then three. Finally I was back at the house. Linwood was there waiting for me. I raced toward Linwood sitting on the porch. By his facial expression, he appeared shocked that I was jogging. I could tell he was trying to get me to stop. I was trying to show off a little bit. I wanted it to appear as though exercise was a part of my everyday life. I speeded up to the house and ran up the porch.

Linwood looked at me with a puzzled look on his face.

"Why are you out here running this early in the morning?" he asked.

"I'm trying to lose weight," I said. "Can't you tell how much I have gained over the years?"

Linwood smacked his lips as if he was brushing off what I said. "It ain't nothing wrong with you, girl! You're in great shape!"

In my mind I was thinking, *Do you see what I see?* He couldn't be looking at this extra cellulite on my butt. Ain't it funny that when Linwood knew me in school, I thought my butt was too small? Now I felt like it was too big! I mean, I had been a size six all my life until two years ago. Now I was a size eight and some tens, and that was very uncomfortable on my body. Nevertheless, I needed a hobby, anyway. Focusing on the positives that were going on in my life had become my new mission in life.

Chapter Thirty-One

I didn't know if it was my new positive outlook on life, or the fact that I had not been on a date in years, but Linwood was more attractive to me than ever. As we ate breakfast, Linwood and I talked about so much. I was surprised at how much we had in common. This was a different attraction. When we were in grade school, our attraction was mainly physical. That was how it was when you were a kid. You knew he looked good, she looked good, and y'all equally looked good together. Now Linwood and I had a spiritual connection. Obviously God wanted him in my life, and he was in it! He made me feel warm and tingly all over.

"So, you never told me what happened when you went to see your mom," Linwood said.

"Well, you know, I practiced forgiveness, Linwood," I said proudly.

"That's my girl," he said. "And don't you worry about old Woody. He'll get what's coming to him. Vengeance is mine, saith the Lord."

I hoped Linwood was right. The only thing I could do now was have faith in God.

"When did Brandy move back home?" he asked.

I began to indulge in my cheese omelet and replied, "Now that's a long story."

I felt a gentle touch on my shoulder.

"Hi, Micah. Hi, Linwood. Long time, no see."

I caught the expression on Linwood's face. He looked as if he was completely shocked. Then a woman, a beautiful woman, hugged me. Even I was taken aback by her beauty.

"You guys look like you've seen a ghost! It's me, Rochelle!"

My food literally fell out of my mouth. Rochelle was a perfect picture of beauty. It was as if God had made her over himself.

"Well, hey, I didn't recognize you," I said. "When did you get back in town?"

"I've been here for about a week now," she said. "Me and my last three kids, we got us a house through section eight. You know I was in rehab for a while, and I got myself straightened out."

"Rochelle, that is so good, because you look amazing!" I said.

I kicked Linwood's leg under the table to get his attention.

"Ouch!" he shouted.

Linwood straightened up and directed his attention to Rochelle.

"Yeah, you look like God has been really working on you," he said.

Rochelle tossed back her long pretty hair and placed her hand on her hip. "Yeah, he sure has. The day Pastor Jacobs and the church congregation came to get me out of that crack house was the day my life was changed. I knew God had sent them to rescue me. I just knew he was not about to leave my children without a mama! Lord knows, I do believe that day was my last hit of crack! I could feel the crack poisoning my system, killing me slowly. Yes, suh, I know I wouldn't be sitting here today if it wasn't for the Lord."

Linwood and I looked at each other. We both knew Rochelle was a walking miracle. This time, Linwood nudged my foot as if he wanted *me* to say something to her.

"Well, I'm glad you're doing better," I said. "Maybe you can come by my house for dinner. Brandy and Ariel are back home now. You should really come by and visit."

Rochelle switched her hand to the other hip. Come to think of it, Rochelle really did have a nice shape. She had always been so skinny, I'd never seen her Coca-Cola bottle shape before.

"Of course, I'll come," she said. "I'll even bring a dish! What time shall I come by?"

"Oh, I can have dinner ready at six o'clock," I said.

"Great! See you then."

Rochelle turned and started walking out the door, all the while twitching her hourglass body as hard as she could. Linwood himself was staring. I tell you what—he may have been saved, but his eyes showed he ain't dead!

After breakfast, we went for a stroll in the park. God has definitely made Linwood into a man. The whole morning, we talked about everything. Not only had I developed an attraction to Linwood, but he had become my friend. Not like we were when we were young, but on a different level. This was a whole new attraction, an adult attraction. A whole new adult love or something like that. I could tell he felt the same way. It was the beginning of something special.

By dinnertime I had already informed Brandy of everything that had happened earlier in the day, and believe you me, she was tripping over how Rochelle looked. Brandy kept asking me over and over again about how she looked, even as we were setting the table.

"Micah, tell me now, do she still have her teeth?" she asked. "'Cause you know, crack rots out your teeth!"

"For the last time, yeah. I seen teeth," I replied. "I mean, I guess she went to the dentist or something. People do that, you know."

I heard a knock on the door. It was Rochelle and her three kids, Sequan, Dylan, and Danielle. She had arrived with a big bowl in her hands. I opened the screen door and gave everyone a big hug. The children went running inside the house, almost knocking Brandy over. Rochelle handed me a huge bowl with foil on top. Then Rochelle put her hand on her hip.

"Y'all stop that running in the house before I get my belt out! Girl, I tell you these kids are full of energy and hungry!" she said.

Rochelle turned her attention to Brandy and placed her hand on her belly. "Girl, you getting fat!" she said.

Brandy backed up in surprise, and then shielded her belly.

"I'm pregnant!" she said. "Thank you very much!"

Rochelle seemed surprised. "Again? Girl, you about to catch up with me, ain't you?" She began to walk off into the living room.

"Wait, Rochelle. What's in the bowl?" I asked.

"Something I owed you from a long time ago," she said.

I peeked under the aluminum foil. It was fresh yellow corn. I hadn't seen fresh yellow corn in a long time. And as beautiful as the corn looked, it smelled equally sweet. Rochelle looked back at me and winked her eye. Grandma Bean had been right all that time. I didn't think that Rochelle had ever appreciated me shucking corn for her, but apparently she had. I used to think she was too high to appreciate anything, but I guess she wasn't. Brandy stood with her arms folded.

"What?" I asked.

Brandy smacked her lips before replying. "I mean, really? It's just corn! Stop smelling it up!"

Brandy walked off, back into the kitchen. I thought to myself, if she knew what I went through just to get this little bit of corn, she wouldn't be saying nothing. And with that thought, I went back into the kitchen myself, because I was hungry!

Dinner was great. It had been such a long time since we'd had dinner in the formal dining room. Brandy looked around the table and then dropped her fork.

"I wish Grandma Bean was here to see you now, Rochelle," she said.

Rochelle let out a deep sigh and replied, "Somehow I think she is here in spirit."

"Yeah," I said. We all agreed.

Suddenly Rochelle stood up and pushed back her chair. "Where is that old tree, Micah?" she asked.

I was startled by this. "What old tree?"

Rochelle placed her hands on the table and leaned toward me. "The one that you and Cherish use to sit under and talk. I used to see you all. The peaceful place—that's what I called it."

I was stunned by this. I never knew Rochelle knew anything about that tree. It was our special tree.

"Rochelle, I mean, why do you want to know?" I asked.

Rochelle picked up her handbag. "Because, I want to go there. I need to go there, now!"

Me and Brandy looked at each other and then answered, "Okay."

Rochelle grabbed both of our hands. "Let's go. Kids! Do the dinner dishes!"

And just like that, we were headed to the tree. It had been a long time since I'd gone to the tree. There were memories that I didn't want to bring up at this point in my life. It had even been a long time since I'd thought of Cherish. I guessed part of me wanted to suppress what had happened, even if it meant forgetting about her.

But God wouldn't let me forget about her. My soul was like a magnet, being pulled toward the tree. It was as if I had no control. The faster I walked, the faster Rochelle and Brandy walked, to the point where we all started to run toward the tree. The weeds had grown tremendously, and the tall grass stained my shirt, but at last, there it was . . . the tree! We were so tired, we plopped down under it. Sweat dripped down my face.

Brandy looked at me like I was crazy. She was trying to catch her breath and asked, "Why you started running like that?"

"I thought a snake was chasing us!" Rochelle said.

"You crazy or something?" Brandy said.

I was in a calm state. Rochelle stood up to Brandy. "Shush, girl! Sit down! Take a moment to at least pay your respects!" she said.

A cool breeze brushed my skin. I knew that Cherish's spirit was here, and then sadness followed. "Why did Cherish have to die?" I said.

Everyone looked at me. Rochelle stood up off the ground and brushed the dirt off her dress. "'Cause she was ready; she was saved. Cherish knew the Lord. There was no doubt about that. Yeah, Cherish was ready. Nothing could separate her from the love of God. Not even death."

For once, Rochelle was talking about the truth. Cherish had been the type of person who didn't have to tell you she was a Christian. You could see it through her spirit. Cherish had a sweet spirit. Brandy seemed to be affected by Rochelle's statement, because Brandy wasn't saved—nowhere near it!

Rochelle slid down beside Brandy against the tree and said, "Which one of us would be ready if God took us today?"

I raised my hand. "I'm ready," I said.

Rochelle raised her hand. "I'm ready too," she said.

Brandy never raised her hand. She just sat there quietly until we left.

Chapter Thirty-Two

I was awakened early in the morning by the sound of a car pulling into the driveway. I peeked out the window to see Linwood pulling his Cadillac into the driveway. He was dressed nicely in jeans and a shirt. I threw on some jogging pants and a shirt. I almost stumbled on a pair of shoes, trying to meet Linwood at the door. Then a sudden feeling pierced my heart. Could it be I was falling for Linwood? I was acting overly excited like a little schoolgirl. My heart felt as though it had sunk into my stomach. I flew down the stairs and opened the door.

"Dang! Can I knock on the door, please?" he said.

I didn't want to appear overly anxious. Besides, when we were in school, Linwood always had a lot of girls attracted to him. So I definitely didn't want him to know I was checking him out. I knew it was silly, but just because you're saved don't mean you change overnight.

Then a car full of white people drove up—two young women and two men. I just figured they were lost. I stepped out on the porch with Linwood right behind me. Actually, they looked rather intimidated.

Then the lady pulled into the driveway and rolled down the window. "Excuse me," she said. "Are you the daughter of Ms. Irish Rose?"

All I could think about was, what in the world did they want with me?

"Yeah, she's my mother," I replied.

"Can we talk to you for a minute about the new developments in her case?" she asked. "We are a student legal team working on her case now."

I was stunned and curious, anxious to know what they had to say. "Sure. Come on in," I said.

Linwood grabbed my arm. "You sure you wanna hear what they have to say about your mom?" he asked.

They parked the car and exited from the vehicle. We all went into the living room. I politely invited the students to sit down and then asked, "So who are you guys, exactly?"

The skinny one with the blond hair stood up in embarrassment and replied, "Oh, excuse my manners. I'm Jamie, this is Amanda, Mike, and Jack. Like I said before, we are from the university law school. Um, we are trying to gain another trial for your mom. We think we have enough evidence to free her."

"Free her!" I replied. I stood up from my chair in a frantic panic.

Linwood pulled me back down. While still holding my hand, he said, "Hold on, now, Micah. Sit tight. Let's hear what she got to say."

Jamie pulled out a box, and within the box were letters—letters that Grandma Bean had apparently written to Mama in prison. Jamie picked out one letter and handed it to me.

"Your mama didn't murder your friend, but she took the fall because that was all she knew how to do," Jamie said. "Your mom was sexually abused by her father, your grandfather. So quite naturally, Woody preyed on her and made her take the fall. It's like a cycle of abuse."

"Now, wait a minute, Jamie," I said. "No one forced her to plead guilty. She thought Woody was going to get her out."

Jamie placed the letter in my hands and said, "She didn't just plead guilty; she *believed* she was guilty. Now, please, please read this!"

My hands trembled as I opened the letter. It was a letter Grandma Bean had written to Mama in prison. I was afraid to know what was in the letter, but I had to know. I slowly unfolded the letter and read it.

Dear Irish,

I can't believe you are in jail. It is truly all my fault. I hate it that Micah is walking around thinking you murdered Cherish. Oh, why in the world, won't you tell her the truth? The Bible says the truth shall set you free. I will not fail her, the way I failed you. When Micah told me she was sure Woody had raped and killed Cherish, I believed her.

No longer will I make the mistake of not believing that evil exists close by. I should have believed you when you told me you were raped. I should have divorced your daddy because of that. So I am not completely surprised that history repeated itself.

But the devil is a liar! I will not have a generation of curses in *this* house! Every day I pray for your soul and Micah's soul. I pray for Brandy's soul too. I have no doubt Cherish is in heaven. Please, my daughter, repent of your sins and follow Christ. That is the only way you can have a good and fulfilled life.

Remember how I used to be? A drunken woman so full of depression? I was too lost in my own darkness to see what was going on in my own house. Look where God has brought me from. If he did it for me, he can do it for you. Well, I have to go now. I can only hope that you will try and restore your relationship with Micah. God knows she deserves a mother in her life. Take care and remember, God loves you, and so do I.

Love, Mom

I couldn't believe what I was reading. I realized that Mama too had been violated! It was all starting to make sense. Maybe that was why she became a drunk. This was all too overwhelming for me.

The student named Mike looked at me, extremely puzzled. He placed his hand on my shoulder and asked, "Did you know that your grandfather had molested your Mama?"

Jamie hit Mike on the knee. "Of course, she didn't know! Look at the expression on her face!" Mike looked at me and began to apologize.

"No need to apologize, Mr. Mike. What I don't understand is what you want *me* to do about all this? I mean, where do I fit in with your plans for Mama's case?"

Jamie came closer to sit beside me. "Well, your mom would need you to testify on her behalf. There was no mention of the fact that you saw your mom kill Cherish. With all the evidence we have, I think we could win this new trial." She smiled.

"So, wait a minute," I replied angrily. "My mom didn't help me, but I'm supposed to help her get out of prison? Oh, no. I don't think so!" I stood up in my chair and shouted, "I think it's a good idea for you all to leave!"

Linwood looked at me as if he could not believe I was acting that way. Before leaving, Jamie handed me a card and said, "Here's my contact information in a case you change your mind."

"I don't think so!" I shouted, pointing to the door.

I slammed the door behind them as they left.

Linwood threw his arms up in the air and asked, "Now why would you go and kick them out?"

How could he get an attitude with me? "I kicked them out because I didn't want to hear anything else they had to say. I'm not going to let anyone talk about my grandmother in her own home. If you don't like it, you can leave too!" I shouted.

Linwood headed to the door with a disappointed look on his face. I really didn't want to even hear what he had to say. I just pointed to the door and then waved my hand as a gesture to get out. Then I folded my arms with an attitude.

"Okay, I get the hint. I'll leave!" he said. "But just know that you can't run away from your past."

Obviously, Linwood didn't get my hint. I really truly just wanted him to leave. Finally, he did. Linwood walked out the door. As I turned to go upstairs, Brandy was there waiting at the top of the stairs. I stomped my way up the stairs. What could she say to me? She couldn't say *nothing* to me! Brandy continued to stand there with her hand on her hip.

"You know, you should have at least listened to what they had to say," she said. I smacked my lips and headed to my room. Brandy was still talking at my door. "If you don't find out the truth, you'll never have a relationship with your mother."

"I don't want a relationship with that woman!" I replied.

With that said, I could hear Brandy's footsteps walking downstairs. All of this news had exhausted me. Grandma Bean had been near-perfect in my eyes. I couldn't believe that Grandma Bean would've let someone hurt a child. I rested my head on my pillow, and pretty soon sleep took me away.

I began to dream. In the beginning, I dreamed of Grandma Bean. I remembered how protective, how overly protective she was with me around people. I didn't know how to feel. I had visions of Grandma Bean pleading with me to talk to my mother. I felt torn. *Dear God, what would you have me to do in this situation?*

Chapter Thirty-Three

Brandy went to church with me, and on a rare occasion, she actually took notes during the sermon. Pastor Jacobs began preaching about old relationships being made new this year. In the pit of my stomach, I felt a nudge, as if it was telling me to confront Mama about what I had discovered. Then I wondered why all of this had been revealed to me now? Why did God wait until Grandma Bean was dead for me to find this out? It would have been easier to ask her, if she was here.

I glanced over at Rochelle—singing, dancing, and praising the Lord—and I wondered why Grandma Bean and Rochelle's mama, Mrs. Sulla, couldn't be here to see her now. Right then, I decided that I would go and see Mama in prison. I knew this was a very difficult thing I was about to do. Mama was a complicated individual. I had never really understood her logic. Maybe this new information would allow me to understand who she was and why she had grown up to be the woman she was. Better yet, it would allow me to see who Grandma Bean really had been, back in the day.

After church, Brandy, Ariel, Rochelle, and I decided to get something to eat. During dinner, Brandy kept going on and on about Pastor Jacobs' sermon and the importance of forgiveness. In so many words, she was hinting to me that that's what I should do. Brandy was always too little too late! Rochelle was just playing along. I guess they thought they were teaching me a lesson. Boy, were they in for a surprise!

I swirled my biscuit around the cube steak smothered in onions and gravy. Sometimes all I wanted was for Brandy to shut up! At some point, I even began to ignore her.

"Hello, I'm talking to you!" Brandy said. She was waving her hands in my face, attempting to get my attention. With the last wave of her hand, I reached up and grabbed it!

"Yes, I hear you Brandy! How can I ignore you when you're waving your hands in my face?" I said.

Brandy relaxed in her seat and said, Well, I was just checking!"

"Besides I had already decided to go see Mama tomorrow. I'm going to see her in the morning. I don't know if I will testify on her behalf. I mean, how do I know she didn't have anything to do with Cherish's death? For all I know, she could have planned the whole thing," I said.

Rochelle gave me the "you must be kidding" look. Brandy smacked her lips so hard, the people sitting next to us were disgusted by it.

"Come on, Micah. Do you honestly believe your mom killed her? This is me, Brandy, you're talking to here. I ain't no dummy!"

Rochelle slammed her drink down on the counter out of frustration. Again, the people next to us became severely annoyed by the noise we were making. "Look, Micah," she said. "You owe it to yourself to know the truth. When you see your mom, at least give her the benefit of the doubt, and see what she has to say."

I folded my arms in disgust.

Rochelle went on. "You can act like you know everything if you want to, but you don't know nothing. Your Grandma Bean and my mama was best friends. Your mama used to do my hair. One day, Mama sent me over to Grandma Bean's house for Ms. Irish to braid my hair. Ms. Irish could braid my hair so pretty and sooo tight! I could wear my style for days.

"Naturally, I was anxious and excited to have my hair done. I ran into Grandma Bean's house looking for Ms. Irish to tell her that everybody liked it. I ran into the living room, the den, and then the kitchen. Then I heard a strange noise coming from Ms. Irish's bedroom. I thought to myself, Ms. Irish snuck a boy home from school, and I was going to catch her in the act and tell Grandma Bean!

"That's when my childhood ended, and my nightmare began. I saw your Grandma Bean with your Grandpa James' hands all over Ms. Irish's mouth. He was on top of your mama doing things no father should do to his daughter! What was worst of all was that Ms. Irish saw me, and her eyes showed no emotion at all. It was as if she had totally disassociated herself from what was going on. A single tear rolled down her cheek. I had a sick feeling in the pit of my stomach.

"I turned around and ran out of that house as fast as I could. I almost tripped over the front porch step trying to get home to my mom! As soon as I got home, I told Mama everything. Then I heard Mama call your Grandma Bean on the phone. I could hear Grandma Bean screaming and crying. I tried covering my ears to drown out the noise, but that didn't work. Mama hung up on Grandma Bean and called the police! Your Grandma Bean came running outside of our front yard, yelling, 'He's going to prison for the rest of his life!'

"The police arrived and ordered Grandpa James to come outside. Of course, he obeyed their orders by coming outside

211

with a gun in his pocket. He wasn't going to prison at all. He slowly came out of the house, pulled the gun from his pocket, and blew his head off! That was the day my life took a detour to hell! I wrestled with that for years. I did drugs because I couldn't get the memories and the guilt of telling what happened to your mama out of my mind. The devil meant to keep me there, but God had plans of his own to rescue me from my own hell—my mind."

I didn't know what to say. I was stunned! I couldn't believe all that Rochelle was telling us. It was a lot to take in. I never knew why Mama had turned out the way she did. I guessed everyone had a past. Brandy also looked stunned. The only one who kept eating was Ariel. Brandy sighed and rubbed her hands through her hair.

"Rochelle, you have really come a long way," she said. "I don't know how in the world you made it!" She leaned over and hugged Rochelle. I didn't know how she'd made it either, but God definitely did. No wonder Grandma Bean had helped Rochelle the way she had. It was all starting to make sense now. And no wonder Grandma Bean had wanted me to forgive Mama so much!

"Rochelle," I said, "Grandma Bean and Ms. Sulla would have been very proud of you."

Rochelle hugged me, and I embraced her back with sincerity. "I think she would be proud of you for standing up for your mom," she said.

I sat back in my chair. I wasn't so sure of that yet. "I'm not sure that's true," I said. "Grandma Bean wanted me to forgive Mama. Some days, I'm okay, and I think I'm over what happened. Then there are days when I'm so angry that I wake up in the middle of the night punching the pillows."

Brandy and Rochelle looked at me as if I were a mad woman. I felt it was in my best interest to stop talking at that point. Rochelle politely cleared her throat before speaking. Then she said three words that would forever change my life.

"Learn to forgive," she said quietly.

"What?" I asked.

Brandy seemed a little puzzled by that statement, but Rochelle leaned toward me and whispered with tears in her eyes, "Micah, you hold the power of when you decide to forgive. With that said, it's getting late. I'm sure Linwood's at the house waiting on you right now."

Rochelle was right. By the time we'd finished eating and driven back to the house, Linwood was sitting on the porch checking his watch. I knew I was late and that he was waiting on me. I really didn't know what he expected from taking me to see Mama. As soon as I stopped the car, Brandy and Rochelle got out, spoke to Linwood, and scurried off to Rochelle's house. They weren't sticking around. I could tell they didn't want to be around when I talked with Linwood.

"Bye, girls!" I shouted. "In other words, I mean *cowards!*" I mean, why in the world were they going to leave me by myself? Linwood came toward me and gave me a big hug.

"Well," he said, "you ready to go?"

All of a sudden I felt sick to my stomach. I really didn't want to go see Mama today. After that talk we'd had at lunch, I really needed to sit down and relax at home.

"Linwood, I don't think I can make it today," I said. "Those grilled onions I ate really didn't sit well in my stomach. I think I'm having gas pains. I was hoping the thought of unwanted gas would detour him away."

Linwood looked at me in disbelief and then replied, "Don't give me that mess, Micah!" He began waving his hands, acting as though he was fed up. "Your gas ain't the problem! Something *is* full of hot air! Something *stinks* around me, and it is *you* being afraid to face your mom!"

"You don't understand what Rochelle just told me," I said. "You don't know what I've been through this last couple of hours!"

"Enlighten me!" he said.

"Okay, but I don't think you want to hear this!" And I began to tell Linwood everything that had happened at lunch. Linwood flopped down on the porch stoop. I sat down beside him. I wasn't sure if I had overwhelmed him with everything.

"Micah, this is why I want you to go and face your mother," he said. "You can't live a lie! You got to start living in the truth. Do she even know that you found out about her past?"

"No. I don't think Rochelle's told anyone else but us. It was very difficult for her to tell us, you know?"

"Of course, it was," he said. "She planted that seed in you; she gave you the truth. Now it's up to you what you are going to do with it."

I sat there for a minute, thinking about Grandma Bean and how Rochelle said she had intercepted her life. I thought about how Cherish had intercepted all of our lives. And the truth was, I cared what Linwood thought. I trusted his judgment. I knew he would not tell me to do anything that wasn't in my best interest. I felt safe with him. I guess that's why I loved him so.

"Okay," I said. "When do we leave?"

Linwood stood up off the porch and reached for my hand. His tall body towered over me, shading me from the sun.

"Now," he said. "We go now!"

I didn't argue with him. Of course, I was kind of hoping he would say tomorrow, but that didn't happen. So off I went in the car, taking what seemed to be a long ride to see Mama in prison. Linwood continued talking the whole ride there. All I could think about was, what am I going to say to Mama? I knew Linwood was talking to me, but all I could hear was blah, blah, blah!

Chapter Thirty-Four

I didn't know which was worse, tolerating the smell of the prison or seeing Mama looking frumpy in her orange jumpsuit. She came shuffling in with a smile on her face. Surprisingly, she seemed very happy to see me. Mama motioned for me to pick up the phone. She looked different, very Muslim-like. Her hair was natural, no chemicals. I'd never noticed, but Mama had pretty, naturally curly hair. I never knew that about Mama. I guess there were a lot of things that I didn't know about Mama. I slowly picked up the phone. *Lord, please help me through this.* I knew it was gonna be tough. I held the phone nervously to my ear. My palms were sweaty.

"Hi, Mama."

"Hey, Micah, I'm happy to see you. Did you get my letters? Is everything all right at home?" she asked.

"Yes, I got all your letters. Everything's good. But, well . . . um . . . there has been something that has come up recently. I've been meaning to talk to you about it."

Mama positioned herself attentively.

"Well, go on. What is it?" she asked.

"I know what Grandfather did to you," I said.

"What do you mean?" she asked.

"He sexually abused you," I replied.

Mama's facial expression changed from happy to sad. There was a state of embarrassment on her face. For the first time in a long time, she had nothing to say. For the most part, I felt sudden embarrassment. I felt a need to console her, which meant, for the first time in my life, that I experienced compassion for my mother. I knew that was from God and not my own free will.

"Ma, it's okay. You don't have to explain," I said. "I just came here to tell you I will cooperate with your attorneys. I'm only interested in the truth."

There was some relief in Mama's face. I wasn't quite sure how much relief I had provided to Mama, though. Well, now was as good as a time as ever to make a run for it, while Mama was still in a state of disbelief. She wasn't talking, and I wasn't going to make her start talking. Actually, I was afraid of what else she was going to say. I didn't want to know how long Grandma Bean knew about it. I didn't want to know how many children my grandfather had abused, nor how many lives he had ruined. So I decided to take destiny into my own hands and gathered up my things. I hung up the phone so quick, it startled Mama. Mama snapped back into reality, and before I knew it, she was banging on the window, trying to get my attention. At first, I pretended I couldn't hear her. I touched the door knob, then turned back to look at her.

"I never asked them to involve you in this," she said.

And with that, I walked out. For I believed, even though she hadn't asked them to involve me, that I *was* involved, from day one. I was involved the day my grandfather chose to rape my mother, when my mother became an alcoholic, when she chose horrible men that used and abused her, and the night Cherish was killed. And now I had to finish it.

217

Nothing could set me free but the truth. I left it at that. The devil had intercepted my mother's life. I could only pray that God would come into her life again. As I was checking out of the prison, I realized that this was going to be a difficult thing to get through, but God always sent us a comforter, and thank God, I had one in spirit and in the form of man. There, sitting patiently in the waiting area, was Linwood. Thank God for Linwood.

I slept like a log through the night, only to awaken to heavy breathing over me. I should have known it was Brandy.

"Well, what happened yesterday when you seen Ms. Irish?" she asked.

I yawned and rolled over. "I don't want to talk about it," I said. Brandy pulled back the covers, exposing my panties and shirt. The cool breeze sent chill-bumps up my spine. Now I was getting irritated. "Why are we talking about this so early in the morning? Why can't we talk about this later?"

Brandy frantically jumped on top of me. I began to wrestle with her on the bed. "Get off me!" I shouted.

"Not until you start talking, Micah!" she replied.

Brandy was bigger than me, so it was hard to wrestle with her and win. "Okay! Okay! I'll testify for her!" I shouted.

Brandy got up off the bed and fixed her hair in the mirror. "Good," she said. "That's all I wanted to hear."

Brandy left after she got what she wanted out of me. I lay in bed, my body restless. For the first time, I thought about the direction my life was going in. I was awakened from my reflection on my life by the phone ringing. Although I didn't feel like being bothered, I was particularly curious about who would be calling me at that time of the day. I answered the phone on the last ring before the answering machine picked up. I really didn't understand why Brandy hadn't answered it.

"Hello."

"Micah, this is Shana. What's up?"

"Up? I haven't got up yet! Look how early in the morning it is!"

"Oh," she said. "I'll let you get back to sleep and call you later."

I rolled over and scooted to the edge of my king-size bed. "Well, now I'm up, so what's up?" I said.

"Nothing. I'll be home this coming weekend, so maybe we can get together and hang out or something."

I didn't know if Linwood was going to come back in town that weekend, but if he did, I definitely wanted to spend some time with him.

"Oh, okay," I said. "Linwood might come back in town this weekend also. Maybe we can all do something together."

Shana paused on the phone. "I mean, what's the deal with you two?" she asked.

I was kind of taken aback by that question. "What do you mean, what's going on with us? We're friends."

Shana smacked her lips in disbelief. "You two have *never* been just friends," she said.

Shana was right. Linwood and I had chemistry between us that really couldn't be explained. I couldn't imagine Linwood not being in my life. No one could ever take his place in my heart. I had always thought I would outgrow him, but instead I grew with him. It was almost as if God set me up with him before I was born!

"Well, I guess I don't know what we are, but when I find out, I'll let you know," I said. "Right now I have to get ready to go to class."

"Oh, that's right! Only a couple more weeks to graduation! I know you must be really happy," she said.

"Yes, I'm excited," I replied. "It feels really good to finish something I started. It doesn't matter how long it took. Chat with you later."

"You too. Bye!"

Chapter Thirty-Five

I had invited Linwood to my graduation from cosmetology school. He was so proud of me that he said yes immediately. I felt like he cared for me, and of course I cared for him, but this was different. This was a grown-up type of love. Oh my God, I just realized that I'd said *love*! I really thought I loved Linwood! Question was, did he love me? He was very supportive of everything, and it felt great to be in the presence of someone who supported me. Everyone around us seemed to realize that we had something special going on.

Time had definitely flown by. I was scurrying around, trying to get things cleaned up. Linwood was in town for the weekend, and so was Shana. Linwood had suggested we all go out to eat. Only Brandy wouldn't be able to make it, because she was sick with the flu. I knew that she was ill, because she never missed an opportunity to eat, and she hadn't eaten a bite since she got sick. Ariel would be staying with Rochelle. I'd never thought the day would come when a child would be safe with Rochelle. Times were changing.

God had definitely brought me a long ways. How I longed for Cherish to be there at times, to witness the new me. Somehow, I felt she was there and that she did know. I didn't even feel disgusted when I visited Mama anymore. Jamie, the law student, was coming to see me in regards to what would be expected of me at the trial. Then I wondered: if Mama got off for this, then what would happen to Woody? No one had heard from him. I hardly thought it was fair that the murderer and rapist was walking around free.

Linwood kept telling me that God would take care of him, but it didn't seem like nothing was happening. He'd probably raped some other little girl and killed her too. It bothered me that he was enjoying his freedom like he hadn't done anything wrong. No one said being a Christian was easy. I heard the sound of Linwood's Cadillac coming up the driveway. I could see him checking himself in the mirror. Ah, he was trying to look good for me. *You know what?* I thought. *He does like me.*

By the time Linwood made it to the front door and knocked, I had checked my hair four times. He knocked only one time before I flung open the door. "Hey, how are you doing? Come in," I said.

Linwood hugged me and made his way to the living room. I followed him like a lost puppy. "I'm doing well. I was hoping you were doing better since the last time we met."

"What do you mean?" I asked.

Linwood looked at me as if I was crazy. "Uh, the last time we talked, you really were having a hard time with testifying for your mom," he said.

I smacked my lips. I didn't really want to talk about that. "Let's go," I said. "Shana's waiting for us at the restaurant." I grabbed my coat and walked out the door.

I tapped my foot, waiting for Linwood to open my car door. He came up beside me and opened it. I politely got into the car and positioned myself. As Linwood closed the door, he mumbled under this breath. "Ornery woman," he whispered. And then he slammed the door.

I shouted at him, "I heard that!"

Shana had already ordered coffee by the time we arrived.

"Hey, guys, nice of you two to show up." I knew Shana was a stickler for being on time.

"Well, hello, and how are you doing?" I replied.

Linwood hugged Shana as we sat in our seats. Immediately, Linwood motioned the waiter over and began ordering our food. That was when I realized how well Linwood knew me. I didn't even have to tell him what to order.

"Yes, ma'am," he said, "I'll have pancakes and bacon, and the young lady will have waffles and turkey bacon."

Even Shana caught on to that. She slowly raised up her eyebrows with an inquisitive look.

"What?" I said.

"I'm just trying to figure out if you two are married or not," she replied.

I could not believe this girl had put me on the spot like that. On top of putting me on the spot, I really didn't know how to answer that. I had known Linwood practically all my life. When I realized that, I couldn't really think of being with no one else. Linwood and I had not discussed in detail how we felt about each other. I knew he cared for me. We were just kind of always in tune with one another, always one in spirit. I watched Linwood gulp up some orange juice before clearing his throat. He placed his glass down and turned his attention toward Shana.

"Yeah, we in a relationship," he said.

Shana burst out laughing. I turned to her in disbelief. I really didn't understand why she was laughing so hard.

"What's so funny about that?" I asked.

"I don't know," she said. "I guess I just don't understand why it took you guys so long to admit it. I think everybody else knew you were in a relationship but you."

Linwood looked at me with a smile on his face. "Do you believe this one?" he said.

Linwood knew he had dropped the bomb on me, and he was trying to pass the buck onto Shana. This single-handedly had to be the best breakfast ever!

On the way back home, Linwood and I didn't say too many words to each other. It was quite awkward to talk about our newfound relationship. It had been so long since I was in a relationship, I didn't even know how to act. We pulled into the driveway. I looked at Linwood. He was even more handsome than he'd been in school. I really didn't think that was possible. But while I had been on this walk with God, he had shown me that anything was possible.

Linwood opened the door, walked me to the door, and said, "Well, I'll call you tomorrow." He turned around and began to leave. I couldn't believe he was just going to leave things as they were. Surely that was a mistake.

"Wait a minute," I said. "What was all that about being in a relationship? Could you explain that for me, please?"

Linwood walked around a bit nervously and replied, "Look, I'm ready for a wife. I'm not looking to just casually date someone. I have definitely been prepared to be married."

Linwood stunned me with his words. I mean, I had feelings for Linwood, and I knew he had feelings for me too. I just didn't think I could have anything I wanted in life. God consistently amazed me.

"Micah, do you hear what I'm saying?" he asked.

"Yeah, I hear you," I replied. "If you're looking for a wife, then I'm looking to be found."

He smiled at me. I could tell he was very pleased with my answer.

"So, I guess we're in a relationship then," he said. He waited for me to answer. It was hard for me to realize that the little boy I'd had a crush on in school would wind up with me as an adult. Linwood had definitely grown up in the Lord, and I knew he could be a blessing to my life. The funny thing was, even when we were kids, it was pure love. Still, it was as if time had never passed between us.

"Yes, Linwood, we are in a relationship."

He smiled, then turned and started walking toward the car.

"That's all I needed to hear," he said. "I'll call you tomorrow on my way back home."

I waved goodbye to him, and before he closed the door, he shouted, "Don't forget to tell me what happens at the mock trial for your mother!" Then he closed the car door and sped off. In all the excitement, I had forgotten the mock trial tomorrow. I knew I was in for the biggest test of my life.

I was running about five minutes late to the courthouse. The babysitter was late for Ariel. Brandy and I moseyed into the courtroom as if we were on time. Jamie and my mom's attorney, Jake Hall, were waiting for us. It's funny, they seemed more anxious to help Mama than me. Mr. Hall was an older gentleman and known to be tough in the courtroom.

"Well, hello there, ladies," he said. "I'm glad you were able to make it here. I was getting a little worried."

I shook Mr. Hall's hand as he led me to the stand. Brandy made her way to sit down. I didn't know what Mr. Hall expected of me. There was a point where I didn't know if I could help Mama, or even if I wanted to. After all, she had confessed to the murder of Cherish.

I sat on the stand and told everything I could remember about what happened the night Cherish was killed. Hour after hour, we rehearsed my testimony. Mr. Hall even told me what to wear to court. He walked from side to side, pacing the courtroom floor. Even though I was there to help him, he had a presence that could intimidate anyone. Then Mr. Hall ran his finger through his balding hair and abruptly stopped.

"So, you didn't actually see your mother kill this girl?" he asked.

I hadn't seen Mama kill Cherish, but I still felt like she was just as guilty. "No, Mr. Hall, I never saw her kill nobody," I replied.

Mr. Hall took his glasses off, then slipped them back on his face and said, "Young lady, did you know that your Mama was drugged that night with a roofie? And that she has no recollection of what happened that night at all?"

Chills ran up my spine. I had no idea Woody had drugged Mama too. In my mind, I could only imagine Mama standing

226

there watching Cherish being raped and killed. I guessed we were all victims that night.

"No, sir, I did not. But now I know," I replied.

God gives you understanding in due time, and with that understanding comes cooperation. I stopped watching the clock to see how long the trial was taking. I just felt a need to cooperate and let God's will be done.

Chapter Thirty-Six

November 22, 2005, was the day that Mama was released from prison and moved back home. Brandy and Ariel had moved out of the house by then and into a rented home on the north side of town. Brandy said it was too much for her to be in the same home with Mama. I didn't know quite what to feel myself. Mama looked like a prisoner in her own body. She rarely went outside of the house, ever.

Rochelle cooked a big dinner for Thanksgiving, and everyone came over. Linwood came to celebrate Thanksgiving with us too. He and I had begun a courtship that was going rather smoothly. I couldn't believe it, but I had fallen in love with Linwood. Our relationship was so close that people would stop and ask if we were newlyweds. Linwood had hinted several times that he wanted me to move to Atlanta with him. When we were married, of course, I would consider it. Shana was even dating someone special. Every time I called her, she would be out with Brad, a producer at the news station where she worked. Most of the time when Linwood came to visit, Mama would shut herself up in her room. Sometimes I think she was embarrassed and ashamed of her life.

It was the quietest Thanksgiving I had ever experienced, and when it was over, Mama and I were left to face each other finally. I stood there, watching her clean up the kitchen. She had lost a lot of weight in prison.

Mama stopped washing dishes and looked at me. "Are you gonna help me?" she asked.

All that time I'd been waiting on her to say something, and that was it? "No, I'm not gonna help you," I replied. "I think I've helped you enough."

Mama looked stunned at my reaction to her. "What do you want from me Micah?" she shouted.

A wave of anger ran through my body. *Lord, help me, Jesus!* If this was a test, I did not know if I would pass or not. Mama stood there with her hand on her hip as if I had interrupted her life.

"Are you kidding me? I didn't have to let you come back here after all you did!" I said.

Mama started washing dishes again. Then suddenly she took the plates and threw them on the ground, breaking them.

"Did you think I wanted to come back here?" she asked. "Come back to all the horrible memories in this house? I feel like I was taken out of jail only to be put into a second jail. This is no kind of life!"

Mama began crying hysterically and shaking. For the first time, I had seen an emotional side to Mama. I couldn't remember ever seeing her cry. Grandma Bean had left Mama $25,000 in her will, but when she was incarcerated it had been frozen. Now, the paperwork had been submitted to unfreeze her assets. Truth be told, the house was supposed to go to Mama. I pulled out the kitchen chair and flopped down on it.

"Well, pretty soon your money will be available, and you can start the life you've always wanted," I said.

Mama wiped her tears away. "I've never been a mother to you. I don't even know how to be my own woman. I've always hid behind some man. I can't even stick to one religion. Do you know there are still parts of my memory that I can't get back?" she said.

I stood back up. I felt like the adult, and Mama was my child. It was true. Mama had never been a mother figure to me. Grandma Bean had always there for me. Grandma Bean had been there for everybody.

"Well, Mama, you have a choice," I said. "You can start living, instead of just being alive."

Mama threw her hands up in the air. "How do you suppose I do that?" she said.

I don't think I'd realized how pitiful Mama had become. She was like a child, looking for a parent. She was like a lost soul looking for direction.

"Mama, you pitiful! You need Jesus!" I shouted.

Mama stood up and looked me square in the eye. "I'm doing just fine without him," she said.

I went over to Mama and looked *her* in the eyes. "If you think your life is just fine, then by all means, keep your life the same. But if you think for one moment that things *could* be better, then come to church Sunday. I mean, really, what do you have to lose?"

With that, I turned and went upstairs, leaving Mama to think about her life's decisions. It was really sad that Mama had lost faith. I hurried upstairs, made it to my room, and flopped onto the bed. That whole experience had been exhausting, but I had a feeling things were going to change.

The next morning when I woke up, I made a decision to just let everything go pertaining to Mama. It took me forever to get ready for church, but when I did, I looked great! I decided to check on Mama. I peeked into her bedroom, but her bed was already made up, and she was gone.

"Mom?" I shouted for her, but there was no answer. I guess she'd gone for a morning walk. Besides, I really didn't have to look for Mama.

As I headed out the door, I noticed something about the house. I noticed that it had become very old. As I walked down the stairs, the floors creaked. The house had held so many secrets throughout the years. I wanted Linwood to marry me and take me away from this house. The only reason I hadn't sold it was because Grandma Bean had left it to me. It was the only other thing I had of hers.

I eased into the church house. It was packed, and there were no more seats near the front. Grandma Bean always said, "Don't be a backseat Christian," but on this date I had no choice. The choir was singing. Pastor Jacobs preached and opened the floor up for the altar call. I closed my eyes at Pastor Jacobs' request for prayer. I could hear the pastor praying for people to come to the altar.

I kept thinking about Mama and how sad I was for her life. I couldn't imagine being as old as she was and not having a relationship with the Lord. How many blessings had she missed out on because she had turned her heart from the Lord? How many wrong decisions had she made, looking for love in a man rather than God? I felt compassion for Mama. I felt that Mama didn't know what it was like to be free in life.

For Mama's whole life, she had just been merely alive, never living. I didn't have any more anger toward Mama. I felt she had punished herself enough. We were like strangers living in the same home. Then I heard the congregation start clapping. I couldn't see who had gone down the aisle to receive salvation. The congregation clapped and started praising God. Then I heard Pastor Jacobs start talking.

"I've known this young lady for a long time," he said, "and I knew this day was coming. This young lady just told me she was sitting in her seat, thinking to herself, what do she have to lose? She then said the answer was, nothing! Church, you don't have anything to lose in God."

Chills ran up my spine. I began trying to see over people. I remembered those words—my own words—but I was thinking to myself that it couldn't be, that it could never happen. Pastor Jacobs asked that the congregation take their seats, and when they sat down, the only one I could see was Mama, standing at the altar with her hands positioned, praising God. I couldn't believe it! I was so overwhelmed that I ducked out the church door. I decided to head over to Brandy's house. I was really feeling like I needed someone to talk to, and since I hadn't seen her at church, I sensed she was available.

Chapter Thirty-Seven

Brandy was sitting outside on the porch with Ariel in her lap. Ariel was just playing away. It's amazing how an only child can learn to entertain herself.

"Hey! Thought I'd stop by to see you," I said.

Brandy was sure something was wrong. She stood up and placed her hand on her hip. Ariel jumped down and ran toward me, shouting my name. Sometimes after you've had a hard day, you can look into a child's smiling face and forget about everything that was going on. Ariel was getting so big, it was hard to believe she was in the first grade. Brandy motioned for me to come in the house.

"Come on, girl," she said. "Tell Mama what happened."

I flopped down on the couch with Ariel lying down beside me. "Well, today I went to church, and Mama . . ."

"I knew it! I knew it!" Brandy shouted. She got up and started pacing the floor. "I knew she was gonna do something else. That's why I couldn't stay there. No, I couldn't stay with no heathens!"

Every time I tried to interrupt Brandy, she would just go on even more.

"And to think you testified for her!" she said.

"Brandy, I—"

"No, don't Brandy me, girl," she said. "I know you saved and got to do what you gotta do, but even God don't like heffas! And she a heffa for sho!"

"Brandy, Mama got saved today."

She flopped down on the couch in disbelief. "Well, I'll be damned!" she said.

Brandy was no help to me. I decided to head home; it had been a tiring day. I actually made it home before Mama did. My body was so exhausted, it felt like dead weight hitting the bed. Mama must have come in late that night, because I never heard anything. In the morning when I woke up, I heard Mama and Pastor Jacobs talking downstairs. I thought to myself, if I didn't move, no one would hear me. I was still apprehensive about talking to Mama about her new salvation.

The pain of liquid trying to exit my body kept me from remaining in bed. Yes, folks, it was time for my morning piss. I slowly eased out of bed and tiptoed to the door. I cracked the door and could hear Mama laughing and joking with Pastor Jacobs. I smelled the aroma of bacon and eggs coming from downstairs. I slowly eased out the door and tip-toed into the bathroom. I even tried to pee lightly, and when Mama laughed real loud, I flushed the toilet.

Then I started to tiptoe out of the bathroom and back into my room. As soon as I opened the door and started tiptoeing out of the bathroom, a loud squeak occurred. *Man, that was loud,* I thought.

"Micah!"

It was over now. Mama knew I was awake.

"Come downstairs!" she shouted.

Well, my cover was blown. I knew sooner or later I would have to face my mom. I made my way downstairs and into the kitchen. Pastor Jacobs was sitting at the table eating breakfast. He stood up and gave me a hug.

"Boy! I bet you sure are proud of your mama!" he said.

Mama paused for a moment and waited for me to answer. "Yeah, that's great," I said. She flashed me a big smile and resumed eating again. Pastor Jacobs sensed there was a bit of awkwardness in the air and tried to make casual conversation.

"So, Micah, I hear you will be graduating soon," he said.

I pulled up a chair and fixed me a plate full of grits, eggs, and bacon. "Yes, sir, I will definitely be finished. Only two weeks until graduation. I take my last exam on Tuesday."

Mama smiled at me. I do think she was genuinely proud of me.

"Pastor Jacobs, Micah is a smart girl. She got that from her father," she said.

Pastor Jacobs was quick to respond. "Yeah, Ryan was a pretty smart guy," he said. "I believe he would have been the finest attorney around if he would have lived."

From what I knew about my father, he was a real good man. He and Mama had dated, and she had become pregnant with me. My dad was very smart and was attending law school. He had planned to marry Mama, but he died before I was born. One day he was walking back from the law library and was hit by a car. The college student that was driving the car had just come

235

from a party off campus. Grandma Bean had always told me my dad dying was the reason Mama started drinking. Now I knew that wasn't the only reason Mama started drinking. Mama's problems had started way before then. Mama took another sip of coffee before clearing her throat.

"Your daddy and I were much like you and Linwood. We were two peas in a pod! There was nothing we couldn't talk about. He was definitely the love of my life. Your daddy used to tell me he would rescue me from the situation I was in at home. I knew the only way your Grandma would let me leave was if I was pregnant. Back in those days, you had to get married if you were pregnant. I felt so responsible for what had happened to Dad that I just couldn't walk out on Ma. When your dad died, it felt as though I was destined to live in hell. Living *was* my hell."

Pastor Jacobs reached for Mama's hand, holding it tight. "The devil thought he had you," he said. "You know the devil is good for trying to make you think you won't get out of a particular situation, but you will. The devil is a liar, and he didn't get you!"

The more I heard about Mama's past, the more compassion I had for her. In God's timing, I was able to understand Mama more and more. "No, Mama, he didn't get you!" I said. "He didn't get you at all. The devil is a liar!"

Mama just smiled.

The weekend came and I was preparing the house for my graduation. Linwood wanted to come down and throw a graduation party for me. I was happy with that, because I really deserved a party. Finally, I'd finished what I'd started; there were many times when I had just wanted to quit. Shana and

Brandy agreed to sleep over and help me clean up. Yep, I finally felt like a winner.

The doorbell rang. I hadn't cleaned a thing. I headed to the door and found it already opened. It was Shana and Brandy. "Hey, girls. How are you guys?" I said. I hugged them both and noticed that, for the first time in her life, Shana had gained a few pounds. I also noticed that, for the first time in her life, Brandy had lost weight. "What's going on? Look at you all! Y'all look different, don't you?"

Brandy and Shana just looked at each other and smiled. Then they both turned to me. "We've got men!" they shouted.

I was puzzled by this. "What do you mean, you've got men?"

Brandy walked over to the couch and sat down. "I met somebody," she said. "He's a policeman. We've been dating for about a month now, and things have been going well. You know, I'm just taking things slow, because that's what saved folks do."

I was in shock! It had been a while since she had been interested in anyone. Brandy had been in her own world. But I was glad she'd found someone she was interested in. Everybody deserved to be happy. And Brandy was definitely happy.

"Well congratulations!" I said. "I'm happy for you!"

Then Shana started twirling around in the living room. She was acting like a ballerina on drugs. "I'm in love!" she shouted.

"Oh God, what's your story?" I asked.

"Well, I met him in the laundry-mat," she said. "My washing machine broke down."

By that time, I'd flopped on the couch myself. "So he doesn't have a washing machine?" I asked.

Brandy burst out laughing.

Shana turned toward me with a straight face. "He just moved here from New York City," she said. She was on cloud nine. And all I wanted was someone to help me clean up. Oh, Lord, it was going to be a long day!

I don't ever remember a time when I was so happy as on my graduation day. I walked across one stage and received my cosmetology license. It had taken me forever to get there, and I enjoyed it. I could see Mama, Linwood, Brandy, Ariel, and Shana smiling at me proudly. Yes, this was a great day, a day that I had dreamed of. To top things off, when we arrived at home, Linwood had a surprise party waiting for me. All of our neighbors, friends, and even Pastor Jacobs came.

I felt like a princess. Linwood and I danced until we could not dance anymore. I realized how much I loved him. After all, I had watched him grow from a boy to a man of God. If there was ever one to be voted "least likely to succeed" in school, it would have been him. Some say that in this world there are the "haves" and the "have-nots." But I believe in God. God can make a "have-not" into a "have." All throughout the Bible, God turned a lot of "have-nots" into "haves." Not only had I fallen in love with Linwood twice, but I had become increasingly proud of him. I knew that he was proud of me too. Linwood motioned for me to come to the center of the party with him.

"Everyone, please, can I have your attention?" he said. "I have an announcement to make."

Linwood held my hand with his palms sweating. I could tell he was nervous, which was very unusual because he was such a calm person. I was puzzled. God, I hoped he wasn't going to move away again. I mean, Atlanta was already far enough.

"What's going on?" I asked. "Did something happen?"

Linwood looked at me and began stroking my hair. Then he turned back toward the crowd. "I said, quiet!" he shouted. Then he turned his attention back to me.

"Micah, we've known each other for a very long time, and God has changed both of us tremendously into what we see today," he said.

I heard people in the background saying, *Amen!*

Linwood cleared his throat and pulled a small box out of his pocket. I was excited, because I had been asking Linwood for a pair of earrings from this store in Atlanta forever. I was happy now. He prepared to open up the box, and I was going to act surprised when he showed it to me.

"Micah, will you marry me?" Linwood asked.

"What? Oh my God, yes!" I was completely surprised. I couldn't believe I was going to marry Linwood. I looked around and saw people clapping, and some had tears in their eyes. Brandy and Shana were crying tears of joy.

Pastor Jacobs looked at me in a very proud manner. Then I saw Mama standing in the crowd. She looked puzzled. I couldn't understand why she had that puzzled look on her face. Rochelle hugged Mama and placed her head on Mama's shoulder. I couldn't believe I was getting married.

"I'm so happy!" I shouted.

Chapter Thirty-Eight

I was still full of happiness when the next morning came. Linwood and I decided on an outdoor wedding. His father, Mr. McDaniel, insisted that we get married in his backyard. Linwood and I saw no purpose in a long engagement. As Linwood put it, "The day I said I wanted to marry you was the day I was ready to be married." So our engagement was to be for only two weeks. Then I would finally become Mrs. McDaniel. Shana was all about planning the wedding, but I did tell her I did not want a big wedding.

Mama congratulated both Linwood and me. Later, I heard a lot of scrambling upstairs and decided to check things out. The sounds were coming from the attic, and the stairs had been pulled down. I could hear what sounded like boxes being tossed and paper ruffling.

I poked my head into the attic to see Mama tossing things around like a mad woman.

"Ma, what are you doing, going through this stuff so early in the morning?"

I'd startled her. She jumped and almost fell into the boxes.

"Micah! Whew, you scared me for a minute there!"

"Well, what are you doing?" I asked. "There was so much noise, it woke me up!"

"Oh, I didn't mean to wake you," she said. "I was looking for this!" She handed me a big box.

"Here, this is for you," she said, "if you want it."

I took the box and opened it up. There was a beautiful, white wedding dress inside. At first, I thought to myself, *Did she buy this for me?*

"This is a beautiful wedding dress, Mama. Was it Grandma Bean's wedding dress?" I asked.

Grandma Bean had been thin enough to fit inside this dress, and I could fit in it as well.

"No," Mama said. "It's not your Grandma Bean's dress. It's *my* wedding dress."

"Your wedding dress?" I said.

I was shocked that it had been Mama's wedding dress. I had never known Mama to be small enough to fit into a dress that size. Apparently, Mama knew I was thinking that. I could tell by the look she was giving me.

"I was that small a long time ago," she said. Mama took the dress from my hands and twirled it around. "Your daddy bought me this dress. I was too shy and to broke to buy my own dress. Of course, we didn't want your grandpa to know we planned to marry. Unfortunately, I never got to wear it; but I kept it. Your dad had this dress made by hand. It's yours if you want it. It's still in perfect condition. I figured you might want something from your father and maybe something from me too.

That moment was a moment I would never forget. I wanted to wear the wedding dress that my dad had given Mama. I wasn't forcing myself to wear Mama's dress just because the Bible says we should forgive. It was a genuine feeling that I had to wear Mama's dress.

"Thank you, Mama," I said. "I would love to wear your wedding dress on my wedding day. This is the most beautiful dress I have ever seen."

"I do love you, Micah."

I really didn't know how to answer that. I loved Mama because God told me to; however, I was uncomfortable with telling her I loved her back. My lips just would not form the words. Mama sensed my hesitation.

"Micah, I'm not asking you to say something back," she said. "I just want you to know that I love you, and I'm proud of you. I thank God every day that you didn't turn out like me. I only wish that I had been a better mother to you. I hope you can forgive me."

I know this forgiveness thing was supposed to be immediate, but for me, the healing process was still taking time.

Brandy and Shana threw a huge wedding shower for me and Linwood. Each day I was packing up stuff to move to Atlanta. We received so many wedding gifts that we really didn't have to buy ourselves much. Shana and I were cleaning up the kitchen from the party, when we heard Brandy calling us. Shana and I ran into the living room. Mama and Linwood ran in from outside.

"Look!" Brandy pointed at the television, and I turned up the volume.

"This just in," said the announcer. "Woodrow Emitt Nelson, better known on the streets as 'Woody,' was murdered today. Mr. Nelson was shot and killed by a father who claimed he had tried to rape his daughter. Apparently, the man was a cousin of Mr. Nelson's."

Mama looked at me, and I looked at her. I couldn't believe it! After all that time, he'd finally got what was coming to him! There was a part of me that felt relieved and another part of me that felt as if he should have been tried in a court of law for what he did to Cherish. I knew he would never stop hurting people until he was dead. Mama looked stunned. I had always imagined that she would be heartbroken if anything happened to her chances of reuniting with Woody. But I could only see a faint smile on her face. She flopped down on the chair next to me.

"It's over," Mama said. She let out a sigh of relief. "It's finally over."

It didn't surprise me that Woody had died by the hands of another man. What did surprise me was the fact that it took so long for it to happen. I knew it sounded bad, but seeing his face on television as a murder victim freed me. He had died with everyone knowing the truth about him. Woody had been exposed for the devil he was. I took Mama's hand in mine.

"Yes, Mama, it's over!"

Chapter Thirty-Nine

So many things were starting to happen for me. I was finally happy. I married the man of my dreams. When I walked down the aisle wearing Mama's dress, Linwood was proudly waiting for me. I'd never felt so happy in my life. Everyone seemed so happy that we were getting married. The whole day was wonderful. It really was the best day of my life. I didn't think it was possible to love someone that much. I didn't think it was possible for a man to love *me* so much.

Everybody needs to be loved. Before Linwood came back in my life, I used to feel like God had forgotten about me. Now I saw that God just saved the best for last. Sometimes it doesn't look like anything is happening, but God knows what he is doing. I couldn't explain why Cherish came into our lives, only to die a short time later. I have learned that we have to enjoy God's blessings while they are here on earth, if only for a season. It only takes a short time to impact someone's life. Cherish's life was an example for my family—that we should live to love and love to live. And that was the way I intended to live the rest of my life.

I was only saddened by the fact that it had taken me so long to reach this point in my life, sad that it had taken this long for Mama to be at peace with what had been done to her. I wondered if she would ever get to the place where she could be truly happy with who she was. There was no more Grandma

Bean for her to rely on to get her through the rough times. I had to admit, I was surprised that Mama had not resorted to drinking after everything that had happened since Woody's death. Mama was used to having a man around.

But not anymore. She seemed genuinely happy for me and Linwood to be married. I worried about whether she could stay on the straight and narrow path. There was a part of me that cared deeply for her, and I didn't want anything to happen to her, despite our history. I guess every child wants a parent in her life, regardless of how much pain that parent puts her through. Children are so forgiving of parents' mistakes. Shana told me I should be focused on myself and to forget about what Mama was gonna do next with her life. But Grandma Bean had raised me right, and she would not have wanted me to leave Mama with nowhere to go.

As for me, Linwood and I decided to leave some old things behind. I thought long and hard about it and decided it was best to leave Mama something of monetary value. Grandma Bean would have wanted it that way. I signed my portion of Grandma Bean's land over to Mama. Now Mama had the house and the land. Linwood and I decided it should rightfully be given to Mama.

When I came back from our honeymoon, I decided to pay Mama a visit to see how things were going. I was anxious to see what she had done with the house. Mama had talked about fixing up the house the last time I'd talked with her. I wanted to see what changes she had made since I left.

As I was driving up to the house, I noticed a For Sale sign in the front yard. Mama was planting some roses outside. The house looked like it had been freshly painted. At that point, I was confused. Had Mama not paid the taxes on the house? Why was the sign in the front yard? Why would she fix up the house only to let the bank take it? Mama came running up to the car in a very excited manner.

"Welcome back!" she said. "How does it feel to be married?"

I got out of the car and looked in amazement at the house. The house actually looked terrific! I didn't know why Mama was so happy, letting the house go when it looked like this. It actually looked better than it had when I'd lived in it. I could tell that Mama had taken a lot of time to fix up the house. I took a moment to gather my thoughts.

"Marriage feels wonderful," I said. "Are you having money problems? Is the bank trying to sell the house?"

"The bank isn't selling the house," Mama said. "The taxes are all paid up. I must say, I put a lot of hard work into this house, and it looks real good. No, Micah, the bank ain't selling the house at all. *I* sold the house." She went over to the sign and pulled it from the ground. "I already have a buyer!"

"You already have a buyer?"

Mama took the sign and headed to the porch, then flopped down. "Pastor Jacobs and the church bought the house," she said. "They gonna make it a recovery house for women and children who are dealing with substance abuse issues. They gonna call it *Micah's House.*

"You know, there are not enough of them around here. What happened with Rochelle really made Pastor Jacobs think about the need for a recovery house where mothers can keep their children and get clean and sober. That's what was wrong with Rochelle; she couldn't stay apart from her children and concentrate on getting clean too. That's just really hard to do.

"Besides, it's time for this old house to produce some good in this world. Yeah, Micah, it's time for me to let go. I always hated this house, but I felt bound to it. So many horrible things have happened here. Why would I even want to stay in it? God gave me a second chance, and I'm gonna take it. Did you know your

Mama always wanted to be an interior decorator? Yes, I had dreams, and now I think it's time to pursue them.

"I think about how old I am and all the time I wasted being drunk and careless with my life. But God is giving me back my time to get things done. Micah, did you know that God can literally stop time? Yes, there's nothing he can't do and won't do for his children. Even me, Micah—even a poor, wretched child such as me. Do you want some lemonade?"

I sat down beside Mama. I hadn't really thought the house would ever leave our family. I was proud of Mama for doing such a selfless act, though. I'd rather that selling it would do some good instead of just being sold to anybody. I was actually very proud of Mama and had an new respect for her because of this. I couldn't believe she had actually recognized a need and was doing something about it.

I guessed Rochelle was happy too. I giggled to myself, wondering if Rochelle would donate some corn to the residents that were going to live there. I could just see her, showing up with a bushel in her hand. God has as funny way of working things out in the end. Mama went to the refrigerator and took out a pitcher of lemonade and poured herself a glass.

"I guess I just thought this house would be in our family forever," I said. "I didn't really think about everything else, Mama."

She took a sip of her lemonade. "This house is a burden from my past. Just a mere shell from my old self. When God delivers you, there are some things you are meant to leave behind. Have you ever seen a baby chick carrying around his eggshell? Or a butterfly flying around with his cocoon on his back? No! When God delivers you, he wants you to leave behind your former self. God doesn't want us to carry the burden on our backs. God has lifted the burden off me, so I can fly, and fly freely.

I looked at Mama, and for the first time, I looked at her with pure respect, love, and yes, even forgiveness. Mama had indeed become a beautiful butterfly. I knew it had to be God who had transformed her into this better person. There was no way she could have done this by herself. I was a grown woman now, and for the first time, I had a total understanding of where Mama was coming from. No one grows up and decides to be a bad parent. There was a series of bad interceptions by the devil, and he tried to make her stay on a bad path. But God had intercepted Mama's path with love that made her go down a good path.

I finally wanted my Mama in my life. I wanted to fly with her in our new selves to a new relationship, to a high that only God could give us. I went to sit over by Mama and hugged her tightly. Mama had finally become the type of mother I needed.

"Mama, I love you."

Mama hugged me back.

"I love you too, Micah."

Made in the USA
Columbia, SC
02 June 2021